# CRASH

## SEAN PLATT
## DAVID W WRIGHT

STERLING & STONE

*To YOU, the reader.*
*Thank you for taking a chance on us.*
*Thank you for your support.*
*Thank you for the emails.*
*Thank you for the reviews.*
*Thank you for reading and joining us on this road.*

# CRASH

# Chapter One

My name is Thomas Witt, and I died twice last November.

The first time was along a winding stretch of road in the small town of Warrenville, New York as we were driving home from my daughter's play. A drunk driver plowed into our car, sending us down a deep ravine.

I was revived by a police officer — first to arrive on the scene.

I died for the second time at Mercy Point Hospital, six days after I came out of my coma and was told we had lost our seven-year old daughter, Kayla, in the accident.

That was nearly a year ago.

They say that time heals all wounds. Sometimes, though, time only carves them deeper.

I focus through my lens on the crumpled red car wrapped around the utility pole. The darkness of night has been interrupted by the flashing red lights and the bright-white headlights of emergency vehicles surrounding most of the accident scene. I follow the trail of debris, exploded from the car on impact. I stop on a girl's backpack, pink with Dora the Explorer, faded and peeling from the back. My stomach sinks as I imagine the girl who owned it.

Of course, I think of Kayla.

I snap several shots, zoom in closer, and see a doll sticking out of the backpack's half-closed zipper — a girl with blonde hair and a plastic smile at odds with the scene's horror.

I wonder if its owner took the doll to school for show and tell. Or maybe she was a shy child who secretly stashed it in her backpack to have something familiar from home to carry her through the day — an anchor to her family no matter how far away they seemed as she sat at her desk.

There's something about seeing the victim's objects that cuts deeper than the rest of the scene. I can imagine the girl wearing the backpack, going to school with a smile this morning, with no way of knowing that today would be the last day of her short life. What things did she worry about? Perhaps she wondered what was for dinner? Maybe she was worried which friends would play with her at recess? Or whether her mother would read her a story tonight before bed?

All for naught.

Her plans for the night, and life, were cancelled by Fate, a cruel fucker, indeed.

The girl was one of two bodies taken away as I got here, already covered in black blankets. Judging from the purse still lying on the road, the other body was her mother, whose own dreams and plans are now also rendered meaningless.

I turn my camera on the massive utility truck that seems to have caused the accident. Other than some front-end damage, the truck looks fine. Its driver, not so much.

I focus on him, hunched over, sitting on the sidewalk, head in his hands, as two police officers stand over him, filling out paperwork and talking to people on their radios. They're now saying something to him. He looks up, and I immediately see his haunted eyes.

He will carry this accident with him, forever.

I snap photos of him, thinking there's no way the camera can capture the lost look of his soul that I'm seeing.

I don't know if he's at fault, or if maybe the car's driver had cut him off, or what. The police can sort that out. Regardless, he's wearing the look of a man who feels responsible for a mother and child dying tonight.

He will never forget this.

I both pity and envy him.

I have no memory of the accident, or the six months prior, that took Kayla's life and put me in a coma for six days. It's not enough to take a man's daughter, but Fate also decided to steal the memories from my last six months with her.

Which is why I started this — whatever you can call *this*: Going out nearly every day, finding accidents to photograph. I can't explain how it began, other than some urge to try and remember, to piece together my own tragedy and take back at least some of what was stolen.

Meghan is worried about me. She lost her daughter, too, but damn, she carries it so much better than I do. The shrink, Dr. Lavender, says that perhaps these excursions are my attempts to find closure. Meghan thinks I can't let go.

I'm not sure either of them is wrong.

When I get home, at 1:40 a.m., Meghan is asleep.

I feel bad that I wasn't there to kiss her goodnight, but she's used to this. Instead of going to bed, I head to my office, turn on my computer, and extract the memory card from my camera.

I load the card into the PC, begin to transfer the

photos, and head to the kitchen to grab a drink while the computer is sorting pics into the new folder with today's date.

I pour tea from the pitcher Meg made earlier, take a sip, and look around the kitchen. A note is on the counter, next to a plate of chocolate chip cookies wrapped in blue cellophane.

The note says:

*"Tried to stay up. Was hoping we could try again tonight. Maybe tomorrow?*

*—M"*

*Shit.*

I forgot.

Meg has been trying to get pregnant for months, tonight was supposed to be the sweet spot in her cycle. We had no problem getting pregnant the first time. Kayla was, in fact, a happy accident. Now, it feels as if Fate is toying with us. Despite many, *many* attempts, it isn't happening. I'm not sure if the problem is mine or hers, physical or mental, but it's giving her too much stress. She's thirty-four, but convinced that her time is running out to have another child, even though we've known plenty of women much older who have had children.

We'd always wanted two kids, a boy and a girl. We had a girl for seven great years. We stopped trying to have another. Meg was pursuing her writing career, just as mine was taking off — again. We didn't worry about it so much. We were a happy family, why mess with what was already working by adding a baby to the mix?

I sigh as I imagine the look she'll give me when I see her tomorrow, just before our certain fight. She'll say, "We were supposed to try!" Then she'll accuse me — again — of not wanting another child. Of maybe not loving her. Or — again — of being obsessed with these accidents.

I hate the arguments. And though I'd never admit it to Meghan, they sometimes push me away from her. Make me *not* want to have another child.

I head back to my office, sit at the desk, and pull up the night's photos. I scroll through them while drinking sweet tea. I usually go through the shots, searching for five or six images that connect to me in some way, which I'll then filter into the collection while the rest will get sent to a raw photos folder.

I make a gallery, rather than scrolling — rows of photos, four by four — to give me a bird's eye view of atrocities, so I can see the threads I might otherwise miss — the story that I know is there, if I can find it.

The sudden smell of Meg's cookies reminds me how hungry I am and of the plate of cookies I'd left in the kitchen. I stand to go get some cookies, but then I see something in the photos.

It slams me back to my seat.

A man I hadn't noticed before, lurking in the background of several pictures.

I pull up the first photo with him and fill the screen. The man is standing off to the side of the road, beyond the police and paramedics, close enough to the scene that he must be part of the crew working it. But he's not in any kind of uniform. He's wearing all black — from his hat to his suit to his shirt.

In the first photo, he's just standing there, staring at the accident.

I swipe the track pad and go to the next photo.

He's still standing there.

I zoom in to see if I recognize him from any of the other hundred or so accident scenes I'd been to. The photos are dark, so he's a bit grainy. I can't make out much other than he's a white guy, maybe in his forties, though I could be off. He doesn't look like anyone I've ever seen. Maybe a reporter?

I swipe to the next photo, then three more.

He's just standing there in each of them, staring at the crash. Normally, a man standing on the roadside might not stand out, especially if I shot many photos in the span of a few seconds. But, as I advance through the set, photos taken over the course of several minutes, he's the *only* person who hasn't shifted position.

I reach the last photo.

My heart nearly stops.

He's no longer looking at the accident.

The man is staring at me.

A cold chill runs down my spine. I back away from the computer, as if he's somehow able to look through time and the photo to see me right now.

I stare at the screen.

I tell myself it's not as weird as it feels.

Maybe he just happened to look up right then to see me snapping photos. I'm sure that to him, and anyone else not used to seeing me at these crash scenes, *I* probably look like some kind of creepy gore hound, snapping photos of the horrific, capturing tragedy for some kind of macabre posterity.

I swipe through to the last photo, and he's gone.

I go back to the previous picture and then forward again, thinking that some time must've elapsed between the two photos, and I simply didn't capture him walking away. But no, that's not it. Everyone else is more or less in place between the two shots. The times in the metadata read only two seconds apart.

Impossible.

I quickly swipe through the rest of the photos, trying to find where he went. But he's not there. He's nowhere.

I return to the photo where he was looking right at me, and zoom in on his face, in all its grainy glory. I save a copy to my desktop, then print it out.

I've made a few friends in the police and fire departments over the past few years, relying on them for some of my research; perhaps one of them can help me identify the man.

I go back and select six photos from tonight, including one of the bodies in black being rolled away, two of the man who was driving the utility truck, one of the doll sticking out of the backpack, one of the car and the field of debris, and finally one of the odd man in black staring at me, and mark them all with tonight's date.

I am about to head off to bed, when, on a whim, I decide to pull up some of the other accident galleries to see if this man in black appears in any others.

My heart pounds as I see him again — in pictures taken last week. As I scroll through more photos going back several months, my heart races harder. I see him again and again, a grim spectator, even in photos taken two counties away.

*How can I have missed him so many times?*
*Who is he?*

I stare at the monitor for what seems an eternity, until 4:14 a.m., when I finally decide I might be able to fall asleep, with the help of pills, of course.

Usually, I worry I'll be visited in my sleep by Kayla's ghost. Tonight, I fear the man in black.

# Chapter Two

I WAKE up to one of my favorite smells, blueberry muffins. It's almost enough to erase the throbbing pain in my head.

Almost.

Sleeping in the corner, on his giant red dog bed, is Gus, our golden retriever. He looks up at me as I get up, eyebrow arched and tail immediately wagging.

"Daddy's up," I say, and he comes over to me and licks my hand, tail wagging harder. He knows when I get up I'll take him for another walk. Gus loves walks like I love muffins. Of course, Gus *also* loves muffins like I love muffins.

I reach for the bottle of pain pills on the nightstand, take one and swallow, washing it down with a bottle of water I keep next to the bed, then look at the clock: 12:17 p.m.

I'm surprised that Meg is baking my favorite breakfast treat. I expected a day of awkward silence and resentment since I'd forgotten about our baby-making session last night.

I get out of bed, relieved, hit the bathroom, then head down to the kitchen with Gus following closely behind.

Meg is sitting with her laptop at the nook table in the warmth and brightness of the sun pouring through the northern window. I look out at the lake and distant snow-capped pines. I can see why she likes writing here. It's nice, open, and inviting, a stark contrast to my own writing space — the dark, cold attic which looks out over the old cemetery just east and downhill of our property.

I notice the basket of muffins covered with a blue-and-white-checkered towel, a side dish of softened butter and knife waiting beside a blue plate. She looks up from her writing and smiles at me, not at all the reception I was expecting. I wonder if I've forgotten some important anniversary or something. It's certainly not her birthday.

I lean down and kiss her cheek. "Mmm, you made my favorite," I say. "Thank you."

I take a muffin, still warm, and dab some butter on top. I lift it to my nose and deeply inhale as I sit across from her. Something about the smell of blueberry muffins takes me to some nostalgic place in my childhood when my mom used to make them every Sunday morning before dragging us to church. Cancer took her before I graduated middle school, stealing my childhood and ending my innocence.

"They're great," I say.

"Thanks." Meg takes a sip of her coffee. An empty plate, aside from crumbs, shows that she started without me.

Gus sits at my feet whining, either wanting me to take him for a walk or to give him a muffin.

"Not now," I say.

"Gus already had one earlier, didn't you? No more, or

the vet'll put you on that yucky *diet* dog food again," Meg says, looking down at him.

He tucks his tail between his legs and slinks off into the living room.

She returns her attention to her laptop screen and is quiet for just long enough to make me wonder if she's focusing on her writing or now giving me the silent treatment. I assume the latter. A new way to drive the guilt in deeper — do something nice, then remind me what a jerk I am by withholding attention.

I love Meg more than anyone I've ever been with, but despite eleven years of marriage, it seems like it's impossible for her to ever just come out and say what's on her mind.

She'd rather stew in her emotions, letting them bubble and froth until they're about to boil over. I can't be too harsh. Given her dysfunctional family, it's amazing that she has her shit together at all, let alone most of the time. We're all products of our broken pasts, it seems, trying to get along the best we can with what we have.

"So," I say, trying to break the ice, or determine the temperature of her mood, "how's it going?"

"OK," she says, still typing, "had a breakthrough on my short story this morning."

"Which one?"

"*Friends Like These*. I finally figured out what is missing — conflict that meant something."

"Awesome," I say, thinking maybe she's not being cold after all. "Want to tell me what you did or do you want to surprise me?"

"Surprise," she says, eyes on the screen, but smiling.

"OK." I take another bite, finishing off the first muffin. I decide I ought to at least recognize my missed appointment last night, even if it might shatter the midday calm. I'm kind of stupid like that, when it comes to clearing the air. I don't know when to leave well enough alone. Part of it is past relationships — my own baggage — and part of it is hating to leave things unsettled. Rather than allowing things to build and build until the big explosion, I'd rather douse the small fires as they happen, and not just because I hate arguing, but also because holding onto shit for too long just makes you sick, and bitter.

"I'm sorry I missed last night," I say, watching her eyes for a sign of what's stirring beneath their placid blue.

Bad sign, her not looking at me. "It's OK. I've decided not to pressure you into this. It's clear you don't want to have another child. I just have to accept that and move on."

"It's not that I don't *want* another child," I say, "I *do*. I just ... forgot."

The excuse feels weak as it rolls off my tongue. Accelerant on the fire. She finally looks at me, and then I see the anger she's been holding in.

"Please, don't."

"Don't what?" I ask.

"Don't lie."

"I'm not lying," my voice way more defensive than I intend. "I've just ... "

"What?" she asks, sensing me fumbling for the right excuse. She's not great at communicating day-to-day, but when we finally do get into arguments, she has a laser-guided missile system that cuts right through my bullshit, and suddenly, *I'm* the one left floundering, searching for the right words.

"I've been busy," I say — the first words to find my stupid lips.

"Busy? Doing what? Chasing accidents to take pictures

of dead people? Because I can't remember the last time you've actually *written* anything."

Ah, there it is — the *real* reason for her anger. This isn't about having another child. Not this time, anyway. She's mad because I'm not writing the next book in our *Dark Family* series.

"I'm trying."

"You've been *trying* for six months. Meanwhile, I'm sitting here trying to keep the mortgage paid. You don't even know how bad it is, do you?"

"Yeah I do," I lie.

"Really? Do you know that we're two months behind on our utilities? Or that our credit cards are maxed out?"

"We've got money coming in," I say.

"Not quickly enough," she counters.

"How is that even possible? We've had the number one book for nearly a year running. Hollywood is banging on our door for a movie deal. And we were on the cover of *Entertainment Weekly* a few months ago. How can we not have money?"

"You only ask because you're not paying attention. We've gone over this plenty. Between the hospital bills and rehab, we're wiped."

"Yeah, but we still have royalties coming."

"It's not enough. Plus, there's some bullshit about 'late reporting' or something that Marty's trying to work out with the publisher. We need to deliver the next book if we want the advance. It's that simple."

"Marty will get it straightened out," I say. Our agent's a pit bull when shit gets thick.

"Marty agrees with me. He says we need to get the book done. We're pushing the publisher's patience, and we could screw this up big time."

I'm surprised. "Really?"

"Yes." Meg's eyes are serious, but I also see their compassion. She doesn't want to fight any more than I do.

She continues, "We *need* to deliver this book. But to do that, I need you to get serious. I need the *old you*. The you from before the accident."

"That me is dead." I'm not quick enough to mask the truth before it escapes my lips.

At this, she stares, as if uncertain what to say. Her eyes are watering. She swallows, thinking, as if cycling through the words that might bring me back from wherever the hell I've gone off to.

I'm not sure what will happen next. Will she give up? Will she grow further frustrated with me, grab her keys and head off to visit her sister upstate? Her sister, Mallory, just had a child, so she's been visiting her more frequently in recent months, helping her out after her jerk of a boyfriend left her the moment he realized the party was over and he'd need to be a man and actually support a family.

Meg approaches, opens her arms, and hugs me.

I feel the pain as she holds me.

"Tell Marty we'll do the movie deal," I say.

She pulls away and looks at me surprised, as I suspected she would.

"But you said you didn't want to make a movie."

"In for a penny, in for a pound," I say with a laugh.

She shakes her head, "No, I don't want you doing this for me."

"You say we're broke, so it's stupid if I don't do it. I mean, shit, I already sold out in the eyes of the fucking literati and the critics, so who cares? Fuck 'em; we need to make money."

She laughs, "This is *soooo* not the Old Thomas Witt."

"Screw that pretentious asshole." I smile as I lean in to kiss her.

Things feel better as our lips press together.

"Seriously," I say, meaning it. "Call Marty. See what kind of deals we can get. Meanwhile, I promise, I'll get back to work."

"Are you sure?"

I nod and kiss her again.

"Thank you." She wraps her arms around me and holds me tight. I can feel the built-up pressure slowly releasing.

I did the right thing.

It's a shame I took so long to finally agree. Whatever was left of my literary ambitions was lost long ago when I agreed to write genre fiction with Meg. Many of the same critics who praised me as some kind of 'wunderkind' at nineteen when I wrote my debut novel, *Shade of Things to Come*, immediately called me everything from a one-hit-wonder to a has-been, to a phony never-was hack when I decided to follow up a decade later with not another stab at the Great American Novel, but a book about a family of vampires, the first in the *Dark Family* series.

I'd traded existentialistic hand wringing for something fun, something I wanted to write with my wife. You would've thought I'd written a book singing Hitler's praises the way the critics responded. Of course, I did myself no favors. When interviewers asked why I'd turned my back on literature, I responded, more than once, by getting up and stalking off from the interview. Suddenly, I wasn't just a sellout, but an asshole sellout, as if money had changed me.

God forbid an author attempts to make money by writing something they love.

And while I had planned to return and write a proper follow-up to *Shade*, it was hard not to get pissed at the critics and the elitists among my fans who felt entitled to tell me what I should write. Worse were the people blaming Meg, as if she'd somehow influenced me to write "trashy pulp novels." Between the two of us, she's far better read and the one more likely to write real literature. It just so happens that we came up with this great idea that we really wanted to write together — a fun, dark series about vampires. I make no apologies for our work, fuck anyone who doesn't get it.

I don't need literary snobs to *get it*.

It's been a while since I've thought about all of this. Since I remembered the anger. Been a while since I felt much of anything, really. I need to channel this anger into the story when I get back to the computer.

Use the haters as fuel.

## Chapter Three

I WAKE up at 9:30 to an empty house, save for Gus in his bed, and a note from Meg.

*"Forgot to tell you, I'm going to Mal's today. Might stay overnight.*

*Will call you later and let you know.*

*I took Gus for a walk at 7.*

*Love you,*

*—M"*

*Good.*

I can use the alone time to put my ass in the chair.

Writing is a lot like exercise. It's a habit. The more regularly you do it, the easier it is. Grow lazy, and it gets harder and harder to get back into it, more so the longer you stay away. Eventually, it gets to a point where everything is easier to do than the thing you *should be* doing.

I sit at the computer, wipe the sleep from my eyes, and look at the file, *Dark Family-Working Draft*, which contains all of our books in the series to date, including the current one.

Last opened more than two months ago.

*Shit.*

It doesn't feel like two months. No wonder Meg is pissed at me. I feel like the world's worst husband. *Dark Family* is our creation in the truest collaborative sense, but I'm the story's lead architect. It's a complicated mess of a narrative, something that's grown more tangled than we planned.

While Meg is a great writer, a better one than me if I'm being honest, she needs me to continue this story. I'm the only one who knows what happens next, and the elaborate backstories of each character that occurred before the series began. While it would probably make sense to create some sort of bible for the series — something she can use to go on without me if I'm stuck in a rut — that's not how my brain works.

I have so much in my head, but there's a lot that I haven't quite figured out yet. That happens during the rough draft — the birthing of the story.

And as I sit down and look at the notes, which are all I have of Book Three, I realize I'm more lost than I thought. There's practically nothing here. So much still in my head, and even more to untangle. To make matters worse, I know there's elements of the third book that I'd planned prior to the accident — missing with my memories. I'm more or less starting from scratch.

*Shit. Shit.*

*Remember the anger! Use it.*

But now I'm not feeling the anger. I'm feeling anxious.

I get up, pace, and figure I'm going to need coffee if I expect to sort this shit out.

I go to the kitchen. We're out.

*Damn it.*

I need to head into town and get some coffee.

A part of me knows I'm making excuses. I can write

without coffee. Another part of me argues, *No, no, I* cannot *write without coffee.*

Just like writing is a habit, so are writing's accoutrements. I'm almost as obsessive as a baseball player. My desk must be completely clear. I need to have exactly two lights on at a precise level of brightness. My music must be going. And, perhaps most importantly, I need my coffee.

While I *could* write without any of these things, it's difficult to lose myself if I don't have them. Working in less-than-ideal situations is like ignoring an itch. Agitation will nag me into surrender.

So I tell myself I'm not stalling, but rather being proactive by going into town and getting what I need, rather than wasting time beating my head against the wall.

Besides, it's not like I don't have the time. Meg will be gone all day, and maybe all night. I can get quite a lot of writing done before she returns — provided I have my coffee.

Yes, I decide. That's what I'll do, I'll walk Gus, take a shower, then head into town. I remind myself to grab my camera — just in case I see any accidents along the way.

Maybe I'll also run into the man in black.

THIS ONE IS BAD.

I know it before I get there, as I see a half dozen police cars race past me, followed by a fire engine and a trio of ambulances.

In my rearview, I see another fire truck, and even more lights behind it.

They're calling out the cavalry.

The intersection of Ash and Culver is blocked, traffic being rerouted by two cops in civilian clothes — they must've been off duty and closest to the scene when they got a call for help. I see the accident just beyond — a tipped SUV, rammed straight into the bottom of a school bus.

My stomach sinks.

I can't tell how bad the situation is from so far away. I need to get closer. I turn as directed by the officer, head North on Ash, stuck in molasses traffic — too many people rerouted onto the smaller street.

I make my first right, turning into a neighborhood just off of Ash, hoping to find another way over to Culver, to get closer to the accident.

My heart is racing as I keep turning into dead ends. Do none of these fucking streets lead to Culver? I finally find one, and see that there's a cop, in uniform this time, blocking access to the street — and the accident.

He's not one of the cops I know, so I don't try to approach him. I turn my car around, head up the street, and search for somewhere to park. I see a house with a foreclosed sign. Grass is high, and windows are boarded.

This will do.

I park, grab my camera, and head through the back-yard and out onto Culver, a six-lane street lined with strip malls, small shops, gas stations, and a few car dealerships. In other words, one of Warrenville's busier streets. I'm standing in a Gas-n-Go parking lot. Several employees and a few lookie-loos are lined up at the end of the lot, staring at the scene.

I walk to the sidewalk, behind the crowd, and pull out my camera.

I focus the lens and see a handful of bloodied, but not mortally wounded, children crying, attended by para-medics. There's plenty of movement — medics and offi-cers — as a few children are carried away on stretchers toward waiting ambulances. Another ambulance rushes off. Above, a helicopter is looking for a spot to land. Helicopters at crash sights are never a good sign.

I find a small boy, face scratched, eyes crying, as a female paramedic is checking him over. I snap a photo.

I scan to take in as much as I can in search for my next subject. My camera stops, frozen on the figures strewn across the ground.

Dead children. Four bodies, with paramedics standing over them.

My gut is swirling, my heart aching, and my eyes watering, I force myself to zoom in, to capture the horror of one child, a boy, dead eyes open and staring straight toward me, it feels, as if begging me to do something — begging someone to do anything.

But there's nothing to be done.

I wonder when the boy's parents will find out, how they will find out. A phone call? A knock at the door? The nightly news? Social media? Nothing will have prepared them for the moment — I remember the doctor telling me about Kayla — that will murder their life as they know it.

I take more pictures, feeling like a vulture feeding on misery for reasons I can't understand. Nothing about this feels good — taking photos of such horrible things. And yet I can't *not* be here. Something about these scenes fills in a part of what's missing within me, shines a light into my murky interior. I feel like I'm always one accident away from remembering my own, and maybe unlocking memories from the last six months of life before the accident.

I pull the camera from my eye, move my way around the crowd a bit. I'm glad none of the lookie-loos are taking notice of me. Because if anybody saw me shooting photos of dead children, they'd probably beat me to death. Even though they're all snapping pics and video on *their* phones.

As I bring the camera back up, scanning the crash site, I see him — the man in black — standing on the side of the street, looking right at me!

The camera slips through my fingers and would fall if not for the strap around my neck.

I grab the camera and raise it, desperately searching for him.

*Where are you?*

I don't see him.

I scan back and forth, but still nothing.

I need to find him. I run across the street, holding the camera to prevent it from bouncing up and down, searching for him.

He *was* standing on the sidewalk in front of a small business center, but now he's gone. I search the parking lot, and see only onlookers staring.

I look up the street, closer to the accident's source and see the back of someone in black — it might be him — approaching the wreckage. I start walking, fast, getting as close to the accident as I can without actually stepping onto the road.

I pull the camera up, scanning the wreckage. I see the bus, on its side, the same line of dead children in front of it, but not the man in black. I look around, searching the crowd of emergency workers.

Suddenly, I see someone looking at me — a big, mustached firefighter. He looks pissed as he barrels toward me.

*Shit.*

I turn around, pretending as if I'm not responding to him. I feel like you feel when you're backing away from a dog while trying not to show fear because that fear is the one thing which will trigger the dog's instincts to hunt you down.

*Keep calm, just walk away slowly. Maybe he won't chase me.*

"Hey, asshole!" the man shouts.

I want to keep walking, but I can hear him coming up fast. Ignoring the fireman might make him angrier. Better to turn toward him and play dumb.

I turn.

He's on me before I have a chance to say anything. His large yellow-gloved hands seize my camera, yanking it from me, strap and all, before I can try wresting it back.

"What the hell are you doing?" he asks, not looking at me, but instead at my camera, trying to figure out the buttons so he can review the pictures, not that he could push anything with those thick giant gloves.

I can't let him see the photos. He pulls one of his gloves off, and his fingers start working the buttons. His eyes are widening at the images of dead children before I can think of anything to stop him.

He looks up from the camera's display and at me, his eyes red and watering. Responding to emergency calls with dead children is hard on even the most calloused veterans. I feel as if he's looking for someone to take out his anger on. I'm the perfect target — an asshole taking pictures of dead kids.

"What the hell is wrong with you? These are people's children!" His eyes are locked on mine, as if eager to take out a world of pain on me. He shoves me. As I fall back, barely able to stay on my feet, he is still advancing.

There's no way in hell I want to get into a fistfight with a firefighter. For one, he's huge and will knock my teeth down my throat. And I've grown rather fond of keeping my teeth where they belong. For two, I completely understand his anger, and don't want him to do something he'll regret and lose his job over. But mostly, I don't want this to turn ugly, though it seems that ship has already drifted from the dock.

I can see my name all over the papers, magazines, on the fucking gossip blogs.

No way this story ends well.

I'm trying to figure out how to retrieve my camera and escape without getting into a fight.

"Listen," I say, trying to explain, "I lost a child—"

He's so fast, I barely register the movement until his fist finds my jaw. Pain erupts through the right side of my face, and sends me to the ground.

"You sick fuck!" he's screaming as he kicks me in the ribs.

I realize just how out of hand this could get. No longer am I worried about how this will play out in the press and blogs. The fireman might kill me. Right here, all because of a misunderstanding.

I roll out of the way, and scramble to my feet. I'm not sure if I'll hit him back or run. I scream, "Wait!"

Suddenly, I'm not alone in my screams. A woman calls out, "Frank! Frank!"

I see Officer Julie Ruiz, my closest friend among the cops I've come to know since my accident.

"What the hell is going on here?" she asks, her voice sharp and cutting through the firefighter's anger. Immediately, I see his face changing. Still pissed, but now, at least, he's thinking.

"I caught this jerk taking photos."

"It's OK, Frank. He's doing a book."

Before Frank can protest, she continues. "He lost his daughter last year in an accident. He's Thomas Witt, the horror writer. A good guy."

Frank looks me up and down, as if trying to reconcile what she said I am versus what he thinks I am. He then shakes his head and shoves the camera into her hands, not mine, and walks away mumbling something about bullshit.

I wonder if she'll look at the pictures.

Julie knows me, and that I won't post these photos on some blog or sell them to newspapers or TV stations. She, unlike even my wife, seems to understand *why* I do what I have to. We've had a few conversations at some of the crash scenes. The closest thing to a friend I've made since moving here, really.

She hands me the camera. "Are you OK?"

The way my jaw feels, I'm not sure if I'll be able to eat for a week, but I don't say that. I just want to get away without further incident.

"Yeah," I say. "I'll live."

"Do you want to press charges?" she asks, though clearly I can see she's hoping I don't.

"No, no. I understand. He thought, well, I don't know what he thought, but I understand."

"Yeah, these scenes are tough, no matter how long you've been on the job. Frank's a bit of a hot head, but a great guy. He's been a hero so many times that things like this, where he's not even given a chance to help, they haunt him."

"No problem," I say. "Can I go? Or am I in trouble?"

"You can go. Probably best that you do since there's some people over there taking video right now with their phones, and I'm sure the press is on their way."

I look along the sidewalk and see that sure enough, the lookie-loos have turned their cameras on me. I'm not sure how many know who I am, but if someone does, there's no way that this won't end up on the news. Then reporters will be calling me for comment, and dredging up my accident and Kayla … again. It was one thing to make the news as a failed Next Big Thing selling out, but another altogether to get the phony interviewers trying to elicit tears by asking my wife and me how it feels to lose our daughter.

Parasites.

I don't want to leave, though, not with the man in black so close. But now there's no way I can stay.

"Hey, do you know this guy? Hangs around the accidents, dressed all in black ... " I try to describe him since I missed getting his picture just before, but the words won't come. My memory of his face seems to lack definition. I swallow, feeling stupid, and repeat myself like an idiot, " ... he dresses all in black. Do you know who I'm talking about?"

"No," she says looking around. "What about him?"

"It can wait. It'll take some time to explain."

"Can I meet you later? Want me to come by your house after I get off?"

"If you can," I say. "Thanks."

"Yeah, shift ends at five, though I might be doing OT with this mess. I'll let you know if I'm running late. Still at the same number?"

"Yeah," I say. "Thank you ... for saving me from getting my ass kicked."

She smiles. "Yeah, maybe next time bring a longer zoom."

"Yeah, I'll do that."

I leave, avoiding eye contact as I head back to my car.

On the way, I hear a woman say, "Is that him?"

A guy says, "I think so."

Someone, maybe the same guy, calls out, "Hey, Mr. Witt!" as I cut through the parking lot, eager to get the hell out of here.

I ignore the man, pretending I don't hear him.

I walk faster.

I want to turn, see if one of these bastards is shooting video of me right now. But I know if I do, I might go full-on firefighter.

Fortunately, nobody chases me. I make it to my car, and get inside. The interior is surprisingly hot for an autumn afternoon.

I key the ignition and flip on the air.

∾

SUDDENLY, I'm in the parking lot of Greene's Groceries, car idling in a parking spot, without remembering the drive that brought me here.

*No, not again.*

I turn off the car and grab the keys, glad to have made it here without crashing into someone.

It's been six months since I've had one of these missing-time incidents. I thought I was beyond this. For a few months after the accident, I would have missing moments — sometimes only a few minutes, other times an entire an hour — gone, just like that. As if I'd sleepwalked my way through with no memory at all. Until now, they'd all been home-based, as I didn't dare drive on my own while suffering from them.

Doctors said it was because of my brain injury, that I was having some short-term memory issues, and that it was likely only temporary.

But now, after all this time, to have it happen again?

*What does it mean?*

There's so much that science still doesn't understand about the brain. Much of my rehab felt like shots in the dark and "we don't know why this works, but it does" kind of therapy. I'd gotten through the worst of it. I'd learned to walk again, and while the months prior to my accident are lost, I feel mostly better.

*Is this some sort of regression?*

I thought this part of the recovery was behind me.

I can't think about this now. And I certainly can't tell Meg, or the doctor. If I do, they'll likely put an end to my daily drives and photo sessions.

They can't take that from me, not when I'm so close to remembering.

# Chapter Four

I'M inside Greene's Groceries, coffee in hand as I stand in line at the pharmacy to get a refill on my nearly depleted pain pills.

Ever since the accident, I've had crippling bouts of back pain three to four days of each week. One doctor suggested surgery, but it's a risky procedure that I can't afford, nor do I want to spend months rehabbing from. I've spent more than enough months, and money, in rehab re-learning to walk, talk, and function again after my brain injury.

As I wait in line, I avoid stares from a woman behind me. She clearly knows who I am and wants to engage me. But I'm not in the mood. I pull out my phone, tap the book app, find a Dennis Lehane novel, and click on the cover, pretending to read. That usually keeps people from talking to me.

Usually.

"Excuse me," the woman says.

Here we go.

I turn and put on my best fake smile. "Yes?"

She's a heavyset woman in her early forties, with thick curly red hair and dark-framed glasses. She's wearing a solid dark-blue dress and comfortable dress shoes. I peg her for a clerical job of some sort. I always try and figure out what people do by looking at them. If I actually talked to more people, I might even know how often I guess correctly. But small talk is tiresome. Thankfully, Meg is much more sociable, or dealing with attention would be harder to bear.

"Aren't you that writer guy … um?"

*Yeah, I'm that* writer guy. *Big fan, eh?*

The weird thing about my celebrity, if you can call it that, is that a lot of people know who I am simply for the work my wife and I have done, but aren't necessarily fans of our books. When you're an actor or singer, people are more likely to be at least passingly familiar with your work. They've probably seen or heard something you've done. With writers, though, there's a good chance that most people you meet don't read books, let alone yours. But when you reach a certain level of fame in a small town like Warrenville, they still know you by face or name. This makes for awkward conversations when people want to engage with your fame, but not because of anything you've done to resonate with them personally.

It always leaves me so uncomfortable.

"Thomas Witt, right?"

"Yes," I say. Maybe she *has* read our books.

"I'm so sorry about your little girl."

Or perhaps she just knows our story.

I nod and thank her politely, eager to return to my "reading."

"I lost my son, too."

*Shit.* I can't ignore her now, or I'll look like an asshole.

I hate talking about Kayla, especially with strangers. I

usually try to let people read my discomfort, and they're usually respectful. But this woman doesn't want to talk about my loss. She wants to talk about *hers*, and I have to oblige, even if it makes me think about Kayla.

"I'm sorry," I say. "How long has it been?"

"Two months ago, his name was Sam."

Usually, at this point, people tend to tell me how their loved one died. She doesn't, which makes me think that perhaps she lost him in a violent or particularly tragic manner that she doesn't want to talk about. Before I can censor myself: "How did he die?"

I want to apologize immediately after the words fly from my mouth, but she's quick to respond. "He killed himself. He was only thirteen."

"Oh, Jesus. I'm sorry. I didn't mean to—"

"It's OK," she says. "I don't mind talking about it."

Well, this woman is a hell of a lot stronger than I am. It's been only two months, after a suicide no less, and she's still functioning, let alone going about her day-to-day, maybe even back to work, judging from her attire.

I feel almost silly, not being able to write — a job that requires me to do nothing more than sit at a desk and draw stories from my mind. It's not like I have to go out and interact with co-workers or customers, pretend that things are fine even as life crumbles around me. All I need is to sit in a room by myself and write, yet I can't manage that. I feel pitiful being around someone so brave with their grief. Suddenly, I'm compelled to hug this strong, incredible woman.

Somehow, I'm able to control myself.

I've been so much more emotional since the accident, I try to recognize the feelings before they overwhelm me.

I can tell by her eyes that she recognizes my raw feelings. She looks at me not like Tom the writer, but like a compatriot in some horrible war.

"He was bullied in school. I didn't see it in time. I mean, I knew he was going through things, but I just chalked it up to the normal middle-school awkwardness. If I'd paid more attention, I might have seen the signs. But we don't get second chances, do we, Mr. Witt?"

"No," I say. "No we don't."

"I'm Kathy." She offers her hand.

I shake it, and say, "Tom," even though she knows my name.

I'm so fucking awkward with people sometimes.

She reaches into her purse, and starts rummaging through a mess of papers, devices, and God knows what else. She hands me a business card, pink, with the words:

*"MEETING FOR THE LOST*

*Have you lost someone? Are you waiting for the pain to ease?*
*Wait no more.*

*Move forward and live again at Together Through Grief.*

*Join us every Wednesday night, 7 p.m., at Academy Middle School.*

*Call 716-555-8568 for more information."*

"It's a weekly group for survivors who have lost loved ones. A mother started it around five years ago when her son got into a car accident and was in a coma. Since then it's grown a lot and has helped me a lot."

"I don't know," I say. "Meetings aren't really my thing. Plus, I wouldn't want to distract people by showing up."

My message comes off a bit cockier than I intend, like: *Whoa, Mr. Fancy Pants Writer is in the room, everyone stop what you're doing and bow.*

Kathy, either not sensing my unintentional arrogance, or perhaps being polite enough to ignore it, says, "Don't worry, no one will harass you there. We're all the same, just trying to heal."

"Thank you," I say, putting the card in my pocket.

"Next," the pharmacy cashier says.

I look and see that she's waiting on me. I turn back to Kathy. "Thanks again. It was nice meeting you."

"You, too. And give the meetings a try."

"I'll do that," I say even though I have no intention of ever attending a meeting. Just what I need, to be surrounded by *more* miserable people. I've got misery handled on my own, thank you very much.

I ask the cashier if my painkillers have been filled. She looks in the *W* bin and says there's nothing there.

"When did you call them in?"

"I didn't. They should be auto-refilled."

She looks on the computer.

"They aren't up for refill for another week."

"I'm out now, though," I say, thinking that surely I couldn't have gone through 120 pills before the month is over. Am I really taking more than four pills a day? I thought I was taking *less* than prescribed, especially since my back doesn't hurt every day.

Maybe I've been taking more, forgetting, doubling doses or something.

She tells me to hold on as she goes to talk to Rajit, the pharmacist on duty. I can feel the line behind me stretching, people's eyes on me, wondering what's taking so long. He looks at her, then at me, as if judging whether I'm some junkie looking to score. I've had a few conversations with Rajit, mostly small talk, and nothing that indicates that he knows I'm a writer.

I wave, hoping he recognizes me. He says something to the cashier that I can't hear, and the girl returns to the counter.

"I can give you enough for tonight and tomorrow, but you'll have to call your doctor's office in the morning and get them to increase your dose if you need more. OK?"

I thank her, then nod at Rajit and smile. He looks at me oddly, and I wonder if he thinks I'm an addict. Weird. I've never done drugs, or even drunk much in my life, and yet I feel guilty like I'm trying to get away with something.

The cashier tells me it will be around twenty minutes or so and to please come back.

I thank her, then decide to kill some time browsing rather than standing around waiting, or talking with Kathy, who is next in line.

Before I know it, I've found my way into the toy aisle, and am flashing back to sometime prior to the accident.

Kayla is six years old, and she's walking next to me, clutching her little purple purse with her six saved dollars, which to her is a fortune, but now, as we're standing there in the aisle of these goth-looking dolls that seem to be all the momentary rage, she's realizing that six dollars won't buy much. It certainly won't buy her the Violetta doll she's had her eye on for a month.

She can buy some small accessories, or save another six dollars or so and get the doll she *really* wants. Saving will mean another three weeks of waiting, assuming she does all her chores.

"Daddy, can I please get it now?"

I tell her no, that she has to wait.

"But it won't be here if I wait, there's only one left!" she whines. "Can't you just let me borrow some money? I promise I'll pay you back. You can have my allowance for the next three weeks. Please, please!"

She drags this last please out a full five seconds longer than necessary.

I want to give in and get it for her, but hear Meg's voice

chiding me in a memory from one of our many arguments. "We have to stop buying her so much. She needs to earn it. I don't want to raise a spoiled brat. You need to be tougher with her, Tom. Every time she flashes those big blue eyes, you cave."

She's right. I do. But it's not like Kayla is spoiled, or anywhere near as bratty as most kids we see.

Kayla squeezes my hand, and looks up at me with such a sad but hopeful look, almost whimpers, "Pleeeease, Daddy."

"Sorry," I say. "We'll have to wait until you have enough."

She starts crying, a last-ditch attempt to get her way.

"Stop crying, or you'll have to wait *four* weeks."

"You're mean!" she shouts louder than she's ever yelled at me.

Now I'm pissed, but trying not to show it. I keep my voice calm, "I know you're angry right now, but you'll appreciate this some day."

Trying to reason with a six-year-old is next to impossible, so I decide to let her stew with her arms crossed in anger, lower lip jutting out, eyes refusing to meet mine. It'll pass by the time we get home, and I'll have shown Meg that I can, in fact, stand up to our daughter.

I flash to three weeks later.

Kayla is clutching her purse, smiling as we get out of the car, eager to get the Violetta doll. I hold her hand as we go into the store, looking down at her, feeling some joy in the happiness she'll feel from working and saving up for something. Yes, she had to wait another three weeks, but won't that make her appreciate the doll that much more?

We get to the aisle, and …

… the doll isn't there.

There are tons of others, ones she already has, and

others she has no interest in, but no Violetta. Her happiness crumbles, and Kayla starts to cry.

I expect her to melt down or say that she hates me, but to her credit, she doesn't.

All she says is, "She's not here."

And I'm crushed.

I would've almost preferred that she yell at me, blame me, ask me why I didn't go to the store and get it for her, then hold onto the doll until she'd earned enough for it — as she'd requested several times. Instead, she's just sad, staring at the shelves as I feel like the world's worst father.

My name on the intercom snaps me back to the present.

"Your order is ready, Mr. Witt, please come to the pharmacy."

And as I look at the Violetta dolls, rows now fully in stock, I'm crying right there in the middle of Greene's.

I wipe my eyes, gather myself, grab a doll off the metal rod, and bring it to the pharmacy. I know it's stupid, but I look forward to bringing the doll back to our house, putting it in Kayla's room as if her spirit will somehow know and appreciate the gesture.

It's hard to explain, but there are times that I feel like Kayla is still here with us, in some form. I've never been very spiritual, nor do I believe in ghosts, but still, at times, I still feel like she's with us in some way. Perhaps it's just me not wanting to let go. But just in case, if there *is* still some part of her here, then I want to give her the doll, even if she can't play with it.

# Chapter Five

I'M anxious and can't write.

It's 5:15 p.m., and Ruiz hasn't called or come by. I'm wondering if she's changed her mind, or, more likely, doesn't want to be bothered with the ramblings of a depressed writer.

I have to say, that since the accident, she's been one of the most supportive people I've known. Ruiz was the officer who arrived on the scene, pulled us out of the car, and started my heart after I'd died.

She was also the one who tried, but couldn't, save Kayla.

We have a shared bond over that grief, different from the one I share with Meg. I think Ruiz has as tough a time getting over the accident, too. That's probably why she humors me, and why she's cool with my showing up at one car accident after another, so long as I keep my distance with the camera and let the cops and paramedics do their jobs. She also asked that I never sell my photos, though she said she couldn't stop me. I explained that I never would, though I am using photos without bodies as part of a photo essay book I'll try to get published once I stitch the pieces of my memory back together. A tough sell: How many people want a coffee table book full of depressing crash photos on display in their living rooms?

*Hey, kids, life is fleeting! I've got the pics to prove it!*

Ruiz has been the only person to show the photo book any interest. I'm not sure if it's because she's humoring me, or because maybe the photos help her deal with shit, too. It must be tough carrying the burden of so many lives on your shoulders. Too much second-guessing. *What if I'd arrived on the scene a few minutes earlier?*

I've played those depressing *what-if's* a million times over. What if we'd stayed home instead of going to the play? What if I'd not been in such a rush, to get home to work? Maybe we would've missed the drunk driver's path by a minute or so.

While I don't remember being in a rush, nor anything from that night, I can tell from her comments that Meg's thought the same thing — that she holds me at least partially responsible for the accident. No, I wasn't *technically* speeding, but I *was* in a rush, driving faster than I should have on a wet road.

What if I'd not been rushing back home to get back to work? What if I'd slowed down to enjoy a few moments with my family instead of been so eager to get on to the next thing?

The what-if game is the worst game of all, because you can't ever win.

The doorbell rings, thankfully offering a respite from what-ifs.

I go downstairs and see Ruiz through the decorative glass in the front door.

"Hey, thanks for coming." I unlock and open the door and invite her inside.

"No problem," she says as she enters, looking around, probably wondering where my wife is. Ruiz is short, has long dark hair in a ponytail, and reminds me of an inquisitive mouse the way she looks at people. She's pretty, though you can tell by looking at her that she's uncomfortable with her looks and the attention her appearances get from creeps. And in her line of work, I'm guessing she deals with more than her share of creeps and their crude comments.

Ruiz has been to our house a couple of times since the accident, as a consultant for our book, which I'm supposed to be writing. Basic police procedure-type stuff so we look like we know what we're talking about.

"Where's Meg?"

"At her sister's. Mallory had a girl not too long ago, and Meg goes to help out every now and then since Mal's jerk boyfriend up and left."

"Ah, nice."

It occurs to me that I have no idea if Ruiz has a kid, is married, or is even dating someone, or if she's into guys or women. While we've talked at great length about our jobs, she's never offered much about her personal life. Despite not knowing much about her, she feels like a family friend. I feel guilty for not knowing more about her. But at the same time, if she's not offered info, I don't want to pry.

She asks, "So, whatcha got for me?"

I go to the dining room, grab the folder of printed photos with the man in black, and hand them to her. "This."

She opens them, and starts thumbing through the pictures, her face confused.

"What am I looking for?"

"The man in black," I lean closer to see which photo she's looking at.

"Which man?" she asks, handing me the photo.

I look closer, focusing on the background, just behind the crushed red sports car where I could swear he'd been standing when I was looking at the photo on the computer, and again after I'd printed it out.

I grab the rest of the pictures from Ruiz and start flipping through the stack, tossing them on the floor in rapid succession as each proves to be absent my man in black.

My heart is racing. Cold sweat beads down my chest and back. What happened to the pictures?

"What the hell? There was a man in black in the photos, in every one of the pictures, night, day, no matter the accident, just standing there, staring."

"Maybe you printed the wrong photos?"

"You got a minute?" I ask, leading her upstairs to my office.

On the computer, I pull up the folders with my guy, and start sorting through photos, my heart beating faster still.

*How can it be?*

He's not in any of them!

I back out of the folders, then pull up the original files I'd downloaded from my camera, working as fast as I can, feeling Ruiz's gaze on me the entire time. If she didn't think I was crazy before, going from one crash site to another, she must be wondering now if I'd just lost the last of my marbles.

I pull up one photo after another, blowing them up on screen, adjusting the brightness, but still — nothing. It's as if he were never in them.

But that's impossible.

"I don't know what happened," I say. "He was in them. A lot of them."

I can feel her gaze heavy on my skull.

I eventually turn and face her. And her eyes scare me. She's looking at me like you would look at a crazy person, whom you must speak to only with caution, to keep him calm.

My heart is pounding. I feel as if someone has doused me in cold water.

And then ... darkness.

I HEAR SOUNDS, people speaking as if underwater, but I can't make out what they're saying. I'm dizzy, unable to move or open my eyes.

... I wake up in a hospital bed, wires running from my body to beeping machines. My eyes are blurry, but I recognize the shape sitting in a chair to my right: Meg.

"Are you OK?" She puts my right hand in hers.

"What happened?"

"Officer Ruiz said you passed out at the house, and weren't responding. She brought you here."

I think of how much this might cost, and my pulse races as I feel sick to my stomach. I try to sit up.

"We can't afford this." I call out for a doctor.

"What are you doing?" Meg puts a hand hard on my chest. "You just passed out!"

"We can't afford more hospital bills."

"We need to make sure nothing's wrong. We'll pay the bills, don't worry."

I wonder if she'd be so confident if she realized exactly how little I wrote while she was at her sister's. A doctor arrives to ask me some questions. Her tag reads, *Dr. Linda Jenkins*. She asks what medicine I'm taking, and how much. I lie and say two to four pain pills a day, even though I'd run out. I don't want them thinking I'm an addict. Worse, I don't want them to cut my meds.

Her piercing gold eyes seem almost unnaturally bright in contrast with her dark skin, and I feel as if she can somehow see straight through my lies.

She asks if I've ever experienced anything like this. I tell her about everything post-crash, leaving out the part about my losing time earlier today.

*I don't want to be in the hospital any longer than I need to be. Just tell me if anything's seriously wrong, and if not, let me go.*

She asks about what happened right before I fainted. I'm not sure what Ruiz told the doctors or Meg, so I tread carefully.

"I was showing Officer Ruiz some photos, and started to feel my heart racing, and a cold sweat."

"What kind of photos?"

Shit. I can't lie, not without asking Ruiz to cover for me, and if I do that, it will make our working relationship weirder than it already is.

"Photos from the crash sites." I leave out the part about the man in black.

Meg sighs.

Dr. Jenkins asks, "What photos?"

Meg answers, "He's been taking photos of crash sites for the past six months."

"It's for a book," I say, quickly before the doc can ask why.

Meg isn't looking at me. I wonder if Ruiz told her about the photos I was showing her. I'm guessing not, or she'd be acting even more pissed than she seems.

Meg says, "Doc, he's become obsessed with taking photos ever since our accident. He seems to think it will help him remember the parts of his memory that are still fuzzy. Can you please tell him that that's not the way these things work?"

Dr. Jenkins says, "Well, I'm not a specialist in traumatic brain injury; that's something you'll want to ask Dr. Merrill."

The doc then tells me that they're going to take some X-rays of my head to rule out a stroke or anything serious.

An hour and a half later, and God knows how much money more in debt, I'm told that the X-rays showed nothing abnormal. That, along with the other tests they'd already taken, leaves Dr. Jenkins with the conclusion that I likely fainted from stress.

She advises me to take it easy.

Meg says, "No more driving all night, taking pictures of crash sites, right, Doctor?"

Dr. Jenkins smiles, "You might want to slow it down a bit, and get some sleep, Mr. Witt. And please schedule a follow-up with Dr. Merrill, as he can better advise you."

"Thank you," I say to the doctor, unable to shake the feeling that she can somehow see through my lies. She looks at me as if she knows about the pain pills, and the missing time, even though it seems impossible. I wonder if the blood tests they did when I was admitted showed an increase of pills in my system. If so, I imagine she would have said something.

～

MEG'S DRIVING us home and hasn't said a word in the twenty minutes since we left the hospital. I lean my face against the cold passenger window, staring out at the passing lights in the darkness because it's easier than breaking the silence.

We finally pull into the driveway. Meg kills the engine, and turns to me.

"Why were you showing crash photos to Ruiz?"

"What?" I'm surprised by the question, and trying to buy time so I can find the right words.

"You passed out while showing Ruiz crash photos. What was in the photos?"

"They were just crash photos."

"No," Meg says, "there's something I'm not being told. I saw it when Ruiz first told me, but didn't think to ask more because I was worried about you. But then, when you were telling the doctor, I saw it in your eyes, too. What's going on, Tom?"

I sigh, trying to buy myself more time, as if she'll give up. We both know better.

I decide to tell her. "I saw something in the photos. At least I thought I did. But Ruiz didn't see it."

"What did you see?"

"It doesn't matter. I was wrong."

She's quiet for a moment, and then asks again. "Tell me what you *think* you saw."

"A man I didn't recognize. I saw him in a lot of the photos, but he's not with the police or emergency crews. I don't know who he is. He's just there. But then when I went to show Ruiz, to see if maybe she knew who he was, he was gone. Maybe I printed the wrong photos," I say, trying not to appear as baffled as I am.

She reaches out for my hand, takes it in hers, and then starts crying.

I pull her close, hugging her, trying to offer some comfort.

"When I got the call that you were in the hospital, I flashed back on the accident *again*."

"I'm sorry."

"I can't lose you, Tom. You can't leave me alone."

"I won't," I say, reaching out and touching her cheek, wiping a tear with my thumb. "I'm not going anywhere. I swear."

She looks up, meets my eyes, and suddenly we're kissing, hands moving over one another with an urgency all their own in the cold dark of the SUV.

She opens the door, gets out (eyes still on me) then opens the side door, and slides into the back of the SUV.

I don't bother with the door. I crawl over the console, pull the side door shut, and I'm on her in seconds, hands reaching up, cupping her warm breasts as my mouth finds her neck.

I hear and feel her hot breath in my ear, somewhere between crying and passion as I slide my hand down the front of her pants and into her.

"Oh God," she says before finding my mouth with hers and kissing me harder, biting my lips. "I want you now."

## Chapter Six

I WAKE to the sound of my daughter's whisper.

"Daddy."

My eyes shoot open, and I gasp for air, woken from some nightmare that I can't quite remember, save for the feeling that I'd seen Kayla again, and that she was talking to me. I'm in bed, cold, the room pitch black save for the alarm clock's light-blue glow telling me it is 3:15 a.m.

In the glow, I see that Meg is sleeping soundly beside me, snuggled in most of the blankets, which she's somehow wrangled from me.

It's not the dreaming of Kayla that's hard. Whether it be dream or nightmare, knowing she's there sometimes when I close my eyes, that I can see her again — even if it's an illusion — is something of a comfort. It's all I'll ever have again, so I'll take it, pain be damned. It's the waking part that's hard.

It's returning to the world absent my child, knowing that those big blue eyes will never meet mine again, that I won't ever hold her small hands in mine, nor hear her infectious giggle.

That's the part that kills — every time.

I close my eyes, trying not to cry.

And then the impossible happens.

"Daddy," I hear her say, soft, as if she's right beside me.

I open my eyes slowly, as if doing so too quickly might destroy what must still be a part of my dream.

"Daddy," Kayla's voice now sounds as if she's coming from outside our closed bedroom door.

I get out of bed, careful not to wake the dream version of Meg. Dreams are fragile, ever more so when lucid and the dreamer is aware that he is, in fact, in a dream.

I must tread carefully to preserve the dream's state and odd logic. It's kind of like those old Roadrunner cartoons. You can run off a cliff and not fall, so long as you don't look down. The moment you do, you plummet to the canyon floor.

I cannot make too much noise; I cannot move too fast; I cannot wake Meg. I must slowly move to the door. But even now, thinking of this as a dream threatens to shatter everything.

*Do not think about it.*

*Do not think about it.*

*Just move forward.*

I reach the door and turn the handle, then step out. At the end of the hallway, Kayla's door is partly open, a pink glow from her lamp cutting into the darkness. And I hear the sound of muffled whispers, barely audible, but talking fast.

I run to her door.

I swing it open.

She's not in here, though.

The room is exactly as it was when she died. Pink walls, her name in purple wooden letters hanging over her bed, stuffed animals lining her bay window with a full bookcase

48

beneath it. The lamp casts the room in a pink glow. I look at her bed, still made from the last morning of her life.

Sitting on the nightstand next to her bed is the doll I bought her earlier, still in its box, just as I'd left it.

"Kayla?" I call out softly to no answer.

I lay on her bed, realizing that I'm not dreaming. I pull her pillow under my head. I can still smell her shampoo, some organic grape stuff that she loved, and I swallow the familiar gulp of pain and regret as I remember lying here and reading with her every night before bed.

Each night without fail, and yet I still feel guilty for all the times I *wasn't* there for her, or for Meg. When work kept me hammering away in my office.

Somehow Meg was able to do it all. Be a mom *and* a writer. I was never able to pull off both at the same time, though. I could either spend time with my family, or hole up for a few months, writing. To be a good father, I needed time away from the words. To be a good writer, I needed to go through the turmoil of bringing things to life in my head. I had to be the aching artist, or the pages would have suffered.

I'm not built like Meg, who can somehow compart-mentalize, and be there for everyone, while still blazing by my word count.

Suddenly, I feel pathetic. Lying here in my dead daugh-ter's room, feeling sorry for myself rather than doing what needs to be done. A poor excuse for a husband and father.

I get up, flick off Kayla's light, and head to my office in the attic, eager to get some words on the page.

I pull up the draft of *Dark Secrets*, the third book in our series, and start typing, not sure where I'm going, but knowing if I just start, I'll get somewhere.

I've got another headache. I take another pill and wait for the pain to dull.

I try not to think about Kayla.
I try not to think about myself.
I try to focus only on the story.

"DADDY?"

I wake with a jolt to the sound of Kayla's voice, feeling as if she's in the room with me. As I sit up and look around at my empty office, with sunlight streaming through the window, I'm dropped back into the reality where my daughter is dead.

My neck and back are aching as I stretch in the chair where I'd fallen asleep.

I look at the computer screen, dark, and move the mouse to bring the computer out of sleep mode. As I wait for the screen to come to life, I worry that I fell asleep and somehow deleted the little work I'd managed to do.

The screen turns white, revealing the manuscript.

Ice courses through my veins as I see what's written:

*"I'm not dead, Daddy.*

*I'm not dead, Daddy.*

*I'm not dead, Daddy.*

*I'm not dead, Daddy.*

*I'm not dead, Daddy."*

It goes on for thousands of lines as I scroll.

*What the hell?*

# Chapter Seven

I'M SITTING in the Academy Middle School auditorium, waiting for the Together Through Grief meeting to begin and trying to focus on anything other than my pounding headache. I took two ibuprofen, instead of my prescribed pain pills, hoping they'd do the trick. So far, nothing.

I look down at the card in my hand, the pink one that Kathy gave me, and wonder how the hell it's come to this. That I need the comfort of other grieving parents to get through whatever the hell is happening to me.

But I'm here, and I can't question it now.

Following the message on my computer screen, obviously something I wrote in a fugue state, I need to do something. I'm sure as hell not telling the shrink about this. I've heard too many horror stories about people being put on pills to dull life. Maybe that helps some people get through the day, but as a writer I think it would cripple that part of me I need most to tell stories. If I can't feel what's happening around me, or if my senses are in some way diluted, what would that do to my ability to put these things on the page?

So, perhaps I'll find something worthwhile in this meeting. If Meg were here, she'd laugh at me. Even when I go and try to get some help, I do it in the least-involved manner possible — sitting in the back row, in the dark, wearing a thick jacket and a baseball cap pulled down over my face so nobody recognizes me, or worse, sits next to me.

I still don't know what I'm going to get out of this. I don't think I'm going to "share" or whatever it is people do here. But maybe just being here, with other grieving people, will help me. Maybe.

I told Meg I was coming, but only because she thought I was going out to look for accidents again. When she asked if I wanted her to come with me, I said not this time. I'm not sure if she believes I'm actually at a meeting, or if she thinks I'm lying so I can go out and get more photos. I did, of course, bring my gear. I never leave home without it.

My phone buzzes, and I look down, then pull the cell from my pants pocket to see a text message from Meg.

*"I love you."*

I type back, *"I love you, too"* and press SEND.

I sit here, holding the phone, waiting to see if she's going to write something else.

Ten minutes pass as the place fills up. There's a lot more people than I thought would show. At least a hundred. I'm not sure why, but I'm kind of surprised that so many people have both lost someone and need the help of others to get through it. Why haven't I ever heard of these kinds of meetings before? Never heard about people I know going to them, or even heard mention of them on the news. Then again, I do tend to get lost in my own little world, or worlds, as the case is with my fiction. Meg sometimes laughs at how oblivious I am when it comes to stuff like politics and local news. If it doesn't directly affect me, or our fiction, I tend to tune stuff out.

Many of the people come in and greet one another, as if they've been coming here forever. Most of them are also sitting up front, which makes me feel like I stick out even more. I don't like when people look back at me, probably wondering about the creep behind them.

I pretend to be on my phone, to discourage interaction before the meeting starts.

A woman stands at a podium on stage, staring out at the crowd. She looks like a soccer mom: well-dressed, relatively youthful, wearing a dark blue-dress, blonde hair pulled back in a ponytail.

"Welcome to Together Through Grief. It's good to see you all. I see some new faces — don't worry, we're not going to drag you up here or put a spotlight on you. This is a place of sharing, but we all arrive in our own time and ways, so we don't want to rush anyone before they're ready."

*Well, that's a relief. They're not gonna drag me up on stage and yell, "Share!"*

"My name is Marcy Harris, and I started this group five years ago when my son, Michael, was in a coma following a car accident. Originally, my husband, Kevin, and I started this group for people who were waiting for a loved one to come out of, or recover from, a coma. But there were only three members at the time, and soon, we'd all lost our loved ones. So we decided to turn this into a meeting for those who have lost someone. As I'm sure most of you have found, it can be difficult to fit back into daily life following the loss of someone who was a part of your everyday world. While the support of friends, family, and co-workers can help, unless these people are sharing your grief, it's not quite the same. Sometimes, we need to talk to someone who's been there. And that's what this group is."

Marcy starts talking about her week, and how she'd thought of Michael several times, but had only cried once. Lots of people in the audience nod along as she tells her story, some crying a bit as she talks. I find myself wondering how many of these people have recently lost someone versus how many have lost someone years ago, like Marcy. And more importantly, does the pain ever go away?

I continue to watch as people take to the stage, telling either their stories of loss, or of how their week was going. The meeting has a weird vibe, somewhere between AA and church, what with all the talk of God and angels and such. Some of these people are sadly delusional, thinking their loved one was visiting them and giving them messages from beyond the grave. They're taking little things, like a light going out in the bathroom, as significant signs that their loved one was sending a signal. Soon, I realize that none of these people have seemed to move on, and I wonder if perhaps these meetings offer more harm than benefit. Maybe it would be easier to get back to some sense of normalcy by not constantly surrounding yourself with people in a perpetual state of mourning, people reinforcing one another's delusions of angels and *signs* from the dead.

I am now confident that this group cannot help me, and perhaps I ought to sneak out now before I hear any more to further depress the hell out of me. Then I see a familiar face — Kathy, the woman from the pharmacy — take the stage.

Well, I can't get up now. If she sees me leaving as she's talking, I'll come off as rude.

I decide to stay as she starts talking.

She's tells the room about the night she found her son, Sam's, body. I wonder why she's telling this story, as I'm guessing she must've shared it before. Is she doing it for the new people in the audience? Maybe she saw me? Or is it something she does each meeting? Is there some sort of catharsis in reliving your worst moment on repeat? Maybe these people are wired differently than me, if *this* is what helps them.

Suddenly, I feel like someone's just stabbed me in the head with a knife. The pain is intense, unlike any other headache I've ever experienced.

I close my eyes tight, trying not to cry out, it hurts so bad. I hear sounds, like movement all around me. But as I look around, I can't see anyone near me in the dark theater.

The pain sharpens. I grit my teeth, riding it out as I reach into my pocket, pull out the good pills, pop two in my mouth, one at a time, and swallow.

The knifing sensation dulls to a low throbbing almost instantly.

I return my focus to the stage.

As Kathy's talking, I notice a chubby boy around twelve or so standing to the left of the stage, in the darkness among the seats. He's all alone, just standing there, staring.

*Weird.*

As Kathy continues to talk, the boy starts to walk toward the stage. He's wearing brown pants and a navy polo shirt, looking kind of like a school uniform. I wonder if he's a student here who accidentally walked into the meeting.

The way he's just staring as he approaches the stage, oblivious to anyone other than Kathy, makes me think he's stoned or something.

I look around and wonder why nobody else is paying attention to the freak show on his way to Kathy.

She keeps talking, "Sometimes, I wonder if I'd only seen the signs a bit earlier, then Sam would … "

She trails off into sobs, and puts her head in her hands as the boy steps onto the stage.

Still, no one is moving to stop him. I wonder if he's with her. Does she have another son?

I'm not sure why, but a chill runs through me — that sense of impending doom like something is about to happen. It's then I notice that the boy isn't wearing shoes or socks. As he approaches Kathy, I can see that he's visibly shaking.

*What the hell is going on?*

Kathy looks to the crowd, "I'm sorry. It's still so hard to talk about."

The boy stops right in front of Kathy and raises his hands, waving them back and forth, but she ignores him, as does the rest of the audience.

*Is nobody else seeing this?*

The boy screams, "Mom! I'm right here! Mom!"

Goosebumps rake my skin as I stare at the impossible, telling myself, no, it can't be — her dead son standing onstage.

This has to be some kind of joke, right?

Or maybe some sort of performance art crap.

The boy continues yelling, but nobody is noticing.

I look behind me, expecting a camera crew or something filming some cruel prank show, but there's nothing but darkness punctuated by the light from red exit signs over the doors.

I pull out my phone, click on the video record button, and focus on the stage, but my camera shows only Kathy.

My hand shakes as I continue to record.

Marcy steps back onto the stage, comes to Kathy, and hugs her. "It's OK," she says, both to Kathy and into the microphone. "Thank you for sharing."

Kathy steps away from the podium, and as she does, walks right through her son.

I gasp, so audibly that a few people turn and look back at me.

I put the phone down quickly and look at it, pretending to be on a call or something, hoping people will turn away from me.

I hear the boy yell, "Mom!"

I look back up to see her walking off the stage, not hearing him.

Marcy starts talking to the audience. "I'd like to thank Kathy for her continued bravery. While talking about our loss does get easier in time, there are moments when it feels like only yesterday."

As she continues, I watch Kathy return to her seat, ghost son in tow.

He continues trying to get her attention, saying her name, trying to touch her, but she's talking with the women sitting beside her, blind and deaf to his attempts.

He breaks down into tears, and I can't help but feel his pain. The notion of a child calling for a parent who can't hear them. I bring the phone up again, turning it toward her, but it still doesn't show the boy.

Suddenly, he looks past his mother, toward me.

I freeze, phone in hand, feeling caught. He turns toward me, now staring as if trying to figure out who I am or something.

My heart is pounding as I quickly look away, pretending to fiddle with my phone, thinking, *Don't look, don't look, don't look.*

I look up.

He's not with her.

He's walking toward me.

I stare back at him, unable to turn away. As he approaches, I feel cold as if the temperature just dropped thirty degrees.

He stops, inches from my seat.

"Hello?" he says.

"Hello," I say, my voice barely there. My heart is racing so fast I'm sure I might drop dead right here.

"You can see me?"

"Yes," I say, seeing hot breath steam from my mouth.

"How?"

I shake my head, just barely aware of my own movements, transfixed by this ghost standing in front of me, "I … don't know."

He asks, "But you're not a ghost, are you?"

"No," I say, wondering if he knows that he's dead. "Are you?"

"Yes." He looks back toward his mother., "Do you know my mom?"

"A little, yes."

"Can you give her a message?"

*A message? Oh yes, I just spoke to your dead son, and he wants me to give you a message.* That *should go over well!*

I can't say no to the desperate look in his eyes, though. "What is it?"

"Tell her it was a mistake. I didn't mean to kill myself. I just wanted to stay home from school for a while. I thought if I swallowed enough pills to get sick, maybe they'd send me to a doctor or something like you see on TV, and I wouldn't have to deal with them anymore."

"Them?"

"The other kids. Just so mean. Please, just tell her it's

not her fault. I wasn't trying to kill myself. She needs to know."

"OK," I say. "I'll tell her."

He stares at me, as if waiting for me to stand.

"When?" he asks. "Please, tell her now."

*Shit.*

*I can't say no, can I?*

I get up and start over to his mother, who is sitting about ten rows up from me.

"And tell her I love her."

"OK," I whisper, not wanting people to look up and think I'm talking to myself. They probably think I'm crazy enough as is.

I can feel Sam beside me, practically pushing me forward. While he hasn't touched me, and I'm not sure if he'd go right through me like he did his mother, I can feel something icy cold propelling me forward, almost like a gravitational push.

I reach her row, where she's sitting on the end seat, take off my hat, and say, "Hi, Kathy."

"Oh," she says standing and hugging me like we're long-lost friends, "You came!"

She pulls away and shivers. "Wow, you are cold!"

I lie and say I was just outside.

She turns to the women she's with and says, "Ladies, this is Thomas Witt."

She says this without saying who I am or that I lost my daughter, which implies that they already know me or perhaps she'd already told them that she'd run into me at the pharmacy.

"I'm so glad you made it," she said. "Do you want to go up on stage and share?"

"Um, no." I look at the stage where a man in jeans and a white T-shirt is talking about his own loss.

I tell Kathy, "I don't think I'm ready just yet. I just wanted to come and see ... " I trail off, not sure how to end that sentence.

Sam says, "Tell her," whispering as if other people can suddenly hear him.

The women introduce themselves as Sheryl and Tanya, offering their hands. I shake them, and then there's an awkward silence.

"Tell her," Sam says again.

But I can't possibly tell her here, in front of her friends.

I lean into Kathy and ask, "Can I talk to you alone for a second?"

"Sure," she says, smiling. Kathy turns to her friends and tells them she'll be right back.

I lead her back a few rows, giving us just enough distance to keep us from being overheard. I look into her eyes, still red from crying on stage, and I wonder how the hell do I tell her what Sam wants me to? There's no way this will go over well. No way she won't think I'm messing with her, or being cruel. No way this won't turn into an ugly scene.

"Tell her," Sam urges beside us.

I look at him, then back to her.

She looks at me concerned, "What is it?"

I swallow, trying to summon the courage.

"I just wanted to say thank you for inviting me."

"Oh, you're welcome," she says with her big sweet smile.

I so don't want to hurt her. She seems so nice.

"Tell her," Sam repeats, this time, louder, like he's realizing that I've lost my nerve.

"Listen," I say to Kathy, "something's come up, but I just wanted to thank you personally, and let you know I'll be back."

"Oh, OK, thank you. Here," she says, reaching into her purse and pulling out a card that says, *Kathy Prescott Candles* on it, and hands it to me.

"Candles?"

"No, that's just a side business I run, I just wanted to give you my number in case you, or your wife, ever need someone to talk to."

"Oh." I look at the card as Sam pleads with me to tell her. "Thank you."

"Have a good night, Mr. Witt." She hugs me again.

"Goodnight."

Sam screams, "Tell her!"

I ignore him and walk toward the closest exit as fast as I can.

He follows, crying out, "Why didn't you tell her?"

"Wait," I say under my breath, "until we're outside."

I push my through the exit and into the school's main hallway, heading toward the eight doorways leading to the parking lot. I stop short of going outside when I see some teenagers hanging around. I can't talk to a ghost out there, so we'll have to stay here and hope that no one comes in.

"There's people out there," I say, turning to Sam who is red-faced and crying.

"Why didn't you tell her?" he yells.

"I couldn't just tell her right there," I explain. "There's no way she would've believed me. I would've only upset her more."

"No, I need you to tell her. *Please,*" he begs.

Behind us, back near the auditorium, a set of doors pops open, and a man and woman start walking toward the exit, and us.

I turn my back to them and pretend to be admiring the row of art projects to our right — paintings and drawings — hanging on the wall.

Sam keeps yelling, "Please, mister, go tell her. You're the first person I've run into that can see me. Well, that isn't a ghost, anyway. Please."

The couple stops a few paintings down from me, also admiring the art.

*Oh come on, just leave.*

Sam continues. "Please, go tell her. She needs to know that I wasn't really trying to kill myself. Please!"

I look at him, squint my eyes, then nod at the couple beside us, trying to tell him, without words, to cool down until they leave.

I'm not sure that Sam gets the hint. He keeps on, getting louder and angrier.

"Please, mister, I don't know if I'll ever see you again. You need to tell her now."

I say nothing, staring at the painting in front of me — a serene lake and a small boat with a father and son fishing — as Sam gets angrier to my left.

"I know you can hear me! Stop ignoring me!"

Lights flicker, almost as if in response to his anger.

"Pleeeeeeease!" Sam screams so loud that I have to cover my ears.

The lights flicker again, then go off.

The woman beside me says to her mate, "What happened?"

Farther down near the auditorium, and outside in the parking lot, lights are still bright.

"I dunno," the man says as he leads her outside.

I hear her comment on something "weird" in the air as they step through the doors.

Now that we're alone, I turn to Sam, but he is suddenly stone silent. His eyes are wide as he stares at something behind me, down the hall near the auditorium.

He swallows and stammers, trying to speak.

I start to turn around, but he reaches out, and I feel his cold hands touch my shoulders, stopping me. "Don't turn."

"What is it?" I ask, wondering what the hell could have him so frightened.

"I have to go," he says. "Whatever you do, don't look them in the eyes."

He turns and flees, racing right through the glass doors and out into the night.

My heart pounding like a jackhammer in my chest, I turn to see what had spooked him.

Just down the hall I see them — six tall, skinny, shadowy things, drifting toward me. Skeletal forms wrapped in swirling darkness, with something almost solid like tattered ribbons floating around them. But it's their eyes that stand out most — large, cavernous bright-white holes in their faces, staring straight toward me.

I remember Sam's warning: *Whatever you do, don't look them in the eyes.*

I turn, heart in my throat, and walk as fast as I can, pretending I never saw them. Knowing somehow that if I run they will descend on me.

*Keep walking. Keep walking.*

I pick up my pace, fighting the urge to turn back and look.

*Don't look, don't look, don't look.*

The doors are now twenty yards away, but feel like a hundred.

Behind me, I hear a disturbing sound — like paper rubbing together — dry and wrinkled, rubbing faster and faster like some sick whisper, or worse, a laugh.

*Don't turn around.*

*Don't turn around.*

The doors are just ten feet away.

The sound behind me grows louder, as if trying to get

my attention. Trying to get me to turn around. It's so loud, I'm certain that if I turn they will be right there, with those empty, bright eyes.

*Don't turn around.*

*Just keep moving.*

I fight the urge to propel myself forward and through the doors.

*Just keep moving.*

I hit the metal bar, which sends the door open, and then I'm out into the night air.

I run.

Past the teenagers looking at me.

Past the couple who'd left just prior to me.

I fumble for my car keys, not daring to look back.

I can no longer hear the sound, but I know if I turn I'll see those things.

I find the keys, open the car door, and hop inside.

I slide the key into the ignition, start it up.

*Don't look, just go.*

I put one hand on the steering wheel — somehow hot to the touch, as if it were sitting in the sweltering summer heat all day.

I ignore the pain, put the car into reverse, pull out of the parking lot, then race as fast as I can back to my home, never looking once in the rearview mirror.

# Chapter Eight

AFTER FLEEING the school like a madman, I finally pull over in front of a Rite Aid and breathe in and out, nice and slow, trying to calm myself.

If I go home like this, Meg will think I've lost my mind. Now, some distance from the school, what I saw feels less real to me. Like I'd somehow imagined it. *Just like the man in black, perhaps?*

Early on in my rehab, the doctor warned me of possible hallucinations. And I did have a few, but they were nothing like this. Sometimes, I'd think I saw something, like a person in the room or a dog that wasn't there. I suppose the man in black *could* be a hallucination, as I've only seen him a few times, and then he was gone — like a hallucination. But tonight was a prolonged encounter with a ghost and whatever those things were. If that's a hallucination, it's on a whole other level.

I know I should tell the doctor.

But I don't want to go back on the pills I was on after the accident to combat some anxiety and anger I had as a result of my condition. They were supposed to help me get better, but all they seemed to do was make me feel listless and made my memory even foggier. I felt like a ghost, half in and half out of this world. If these hallucinations are indicative of some sort of mental problem, I don't want to be put back on those pills and lose myself again.

I can't tell Meg or the doctor.

Not yet. Not when I feel like these things might be happening for a reason. I can't help but feel like they're helping me get closer to my missing memories. Perhaps it's my damaged brain's way of piecing things together. If I can just ride them out a bit longer, I'll remember everything, and perhaps finally have some peace.

I reach into my pocket, fish out two pain pills, and swallow.

I go inside the store, and pick up a bottle of water and a newspaper, figuring I'll chill for a bit in the parking lot while waiting for the pills to do their magic.

They do more than dim the pain; pills calm my manic thoughts, and promise a joy I don't otherwise feel. When I was younger, I remember hearing about how the singer of Nirvana, Kurt Cobain, had killed himself. At the time, I couldn't understand how someone with so much success could become addicted to heroin. Why would anyone choose to flush their life away like that? A few days into my pills, an opiate not close to as powerful as heroin, it suddenly made sense.

I can now see why someone can get so easily hooked.

I wonder if I'm a junkie for loving the pills so much, then figure if I'm wondering then I probably am. Yes, I have real pain, a holdover from my accident, but how often do I just take the pills to ease my mind or feel better? More than I'm willing to admit to anyone else.

I return to my car, paper in hand, and flick on the lights just above the rearview mirror.

I unfold the sports page and prepare to kill time while waiting for the happy feeling to kick in. About four stories in, I'm surprised to feel that familiar rush runs through me so soon.

And with it, comes something else: a flash of memory.

I'm in the car, driving. It's still light outside, though the sun is setting. Meg is beside me. Kayla's in the back seat, singing some song that's playing on the CD player. The song, I suddenly remember, that she was practicing for her school play!

This must be a memory from that night.

Still in the memory, I look back at Kayla. She meets my eyes in the rearview. She feels so real that I want to reach back and hug her, but I know that if I move or open my eyes, the memory will pop like a bubble floating through the night.

As I'm looking at her, I notice a blur beside her in the back seat. Bright, almost like a lens flare you'd see in a photograph. Something about it is bothering me like an itch just under my skin.

*What is that?*

Still in the memory, I reach up to adjust the mirror and get a better look.

And as I do, the bubble pops. I'm back in the Rite Aid parking lot, crying.

I feel closer than ever to remembering the accident.

I look down at the pill bottle and connect the dots. I'm not sure how I know, or if it's just an addict's wishful thinking, but I realize that the pills may provide a shortcut to remembering that night.

~

As I PULL up to my house and go through the gates, I notice an unfamiliar car in the driveway: a black Lexus.

I look up to the house to see the dining room light on, and two shapes behind the curtains, moving. Why the hell didn't Meg tell me we were having company tonight? I don't have time for company. And I need to tell her what happened, not sit and play like nothing's wrong for three hours while we entertain someone I don't want to talk to.

I sit in the car and try to calm my rising anxiety.

I take one more pill, even though I just took two less than twenty minutes ago.

I get out of the car, close my eyes, and breathe in the cool, fresh breeze. Leaves scrape across the semicircle cobblestone driveway as I look up the road for anything out of the ordinary — any sign of those things, whatever they were.

We live on a cul de sac on a small hill overlooking the town. There are only four other houses on our quiet street, each of them also behind gates. The Sandersons, who live two doors down on the west side of the street, have their grandkids over, and there's music wafting from their yard, but nothing out of the ordinary, and certainly no sign of ghosts.

As I sit on my calm street, what happened at the school seems like another lifetime ago. Everything feels fine now, which reaffirms my decision to keep it all to myself.

If I go in there and tell her the truth, she'll probably call the doctor. Hell, she could even have me admitted to the psych ward.

Even if she didn't go that far, she certainly wouldn't let me out alone again. She'll start to worry about me — again — like some sort of child or invalid. And right now, she needs me to be strong. She needs me to finish this damned book so we can pay our bills and get back to trying to start a family.

I remind myself to research hallucinations later, perhaps see if they're among the side effects of the pain pills. If so, maybe the doc can prescribe something else. Though if these pills are in fact helping me to remember the accident, there's no way in hell I'm going to give them up.

I'll take hallucinations all day every day if they help me put the pieces of my life back together.

I look out the gate at the street again, hearing the sounds of children laughing and think of Kayla, then head inside to meet our guest.

~

I HEAR MY NAME, or a familiar bastardization of it, as I swing open the door.

"Tommy!"

Only one person gets away with calling me "Tommy": my agent, Marty.

As I step into the dining room, he lifts his large frame out of the seat and comes over to give me a giant bear hug, big enough to almost swallow me. Marty, at six foot five, towers over me, and outweighs me by at least a buck fifty.

"How's it going, buddy? You look good, well, for a skinny bastard," he says with a laugh as he lets me go, looking me up and down like he hasn't seen me in forever. I suppose it has been forever, relatively speaking. Last time we spoke in person, I was in rehab following the coma, still bruised, putting one foot in front of another, re-learning how to walk.

"Good, good," I say, trying to figure out why he's here.

Then I remember that Meg and I had talked about

having him get us a movie deal. Maybe he's here with good news? Or perhaps just to see what we're looking for? Either way, I welcome the distraction. Marty is one of the few people who can make life seem normal again. And if somehow those ghost things *are* real and tried to come in our house, Marty would be the kind of guy I'd want by my side to send them right back to hell.

Meg comes over and kisses me, then asks how the meeting went.

"Fine," I say, hoping she can't sense the lie behind my lips.

I inhale deeply, realizing that she's made my favorite: linguine and meatballs with garlic bread.

"Dinner's almost done, you two sit down and catch up," she says, heading back into the kitchen. Marty sits back down at the dinner table and takes a sip from his wine before he pours a glass for me from a bottle of Tignanello, which I assume he brought with him.

"We celebrating something?" I ask as I take a seat opposite him, leaving a spot at the head of the table for Meg.

"Might be," he says with a sly grin. "I already told Meg, but I talked with a guy, Russell Thompson, ring a bell?"

"Should it?" I ask.

"He's the new head over at Infinity Studios. They have deals with three networks, and he's pretty sure he can make a *Dark Family* series a reality at either AMC or HBO, or hell, even ABC if you want to water it down."

"Really?" I say, taking a sip of the wine. Usually, I can't tell the difference between the cheap stuff Meg sometimes gets and the ridiculous bottles that Marty brings over, but this one is good. Almost soft, pleasant to swallow. I take another sip.

"Good shit, eh?" he says, noticing my second drink.

"Yeah, yeah," I say. "I don't even wanna know how much this one costs."

"Well, let's just say we wouldn't be drinking it if I didn't have good news. Aw, who am I kidding, there's always a reason to celebrate if you think hard enough."

"So," I say, "what do I need to do to make this happen?"

"Write out a proposal I can pitch to him. We talked briefly, and he knows who you both are and of your series, but doesn't know dick about it save for the buzz. You write something up, and I'll have Johnny K spiff it up."

Johnny K was one of the script doctors Marty worked with, brought in to punch up screenplays. Novels and scripts were different beasts. And while many writers can learn to write both, I have zero interest in learning scriptwriting when I'd rather focus on books.

"Yeah," I say, "that works for me. When do you need it by?"

"In two days?"

"Jesus, short enough notice, Marty?"

"Sorry, but I'm flying in to meet Russell about something else, and if you want this to happen sooner rather than later, I need something now."

Meg comes in with a large bowl of steaming linguini with just a bit of marinara and a light coating of butter, just how I like it. She then returns with two bowls, one with plump meatballs — her meatballs are the best I've ever had — and a second bowl of garlic bread. My stomach rumbles in anticipation as she sits.

"This looks, and smells, delicious, Meg," Marty says. "Been so long since I've had a decent home-cooked meal."

"Well, I'm sure it's not as good as the restaurants you usually eat at, but … "

"Nonsense," he says, loading his plate with pasta. "Those places got nothin' on the love you put into this."

Meg laughed, "Yes, love and two jars of store-brand marinara."

~

AFTER DINNER, Meg excuses herself to call her sister, Mallory, which seems like a convenient and obvious way to give Marty and me some alone time. Clearly, she'd told him what was going on, and now he was going to start asking me if I was OK, or had gone full mental as Meg probably suspected.

We're standing outside on the deck looking out over the lake behind the house. To the right and downhill, is the old church and cemetery. To the left, more woods. Above, the moon peered out from behind fast-moving clouds, painting the sky a beautiful shade of violet. Times like this, I'm glad I left the South Florida rat race, trading near-constant sun for scenery and seasons.

"So," Marty says, winding his pitch, "Meg says you've lost your mind."

I shake my head with a grin. "Ever the subtle segue, Marty."

"Hey, if you want subtle, hire someone else. We're friends, right, Tommy? And I don't mince words or dance with friends. I cut to the chase, so why don't you do the same? What's going on?"

"Nothing," I say, about as convincing as a dog begging to have his balls cut.

"Don't bullshit a bullshitter, Tommy. What's going on? You steppin' out on Meg or something? If so, that's your business, even though I'd have to tell you you're a flippin' idiot."

"No, I'm not cheating on Meg," I say, pissed he'd even suggest such a thing. "Besides, *you* are the last person in the world with the right to preach about that."

I didn't need to finish the thought by citing Marty's three ex-wives or six children with four women.

Marty held up his hands, shaking his head back and forth, "Hey, hey, hey, have some respect. I wasn't accusing you of anything. Your wife is worried about you, and even though you and I go way back, Meg's my client, too, and I'd not be doing my job if I didn't try to get to the bottom of this. So, tell me, what's going on?"

I start with the man in the photos, and how he vanished, to see how Marty reacts, before deciding if I'll tell him about what happened tonight with the ghost and those weird things.

After I tell him about the man in black, and how Officer Ruiz didn't see him in the photos, Marty asks, "What are these pills you're taking?"

I tell him.

"Yes, they can cause hallucinations. You need to have the doc prescribe you something else. But there's also other causes for hallucinations, far more troublesome causes related to your injury, including psychosis in some people. This isn't something you should be fucking around with, considering your accident. You need to get to your doctors and sort it all out."

"I know," I say, deciding not to tell him about the school or the Kayla incident.

"Tell me you're going to talk to your doctor."

"I will," I promise.

# Chapter Nine

I'M SITTING in Dr. Merrill's office, following an MRI scan, watching as he looks over the results on his computer. Pictures of the insides of my skull are on an overhead screen behind him.

"There's nothing indicative of a problem on your scans," he says. "How often are the hallucinations occurring?"

"Not often," I say. "Just a few here and there."

I've not been totally forthcoming with the doctor. While I told him about my "hallucinations" of the man in black, I've not told him about hearing Kayla's voice, her "message," or what happened at the auditorium. I figure if something's wrong, he'll see it on the MRI. No need to tell him about all the things I've seen.

For one, I don't want him thinking I'm crazy. For two, I don't want anyone cutting my pills.

"How about headaches? Are you getting headaches?"

While I hadn't given much thought to it before, I remember the splitting headache I had in the auditorium just before I saw Sam. And there'd been a few others, lately.

"Yeah," I say. "Now that you mention it. Does it mean anything?"

"How often are you having them? And how bad are they?"

"Not often," I say. "Mostly, they're like migraines I used to get. One night was really bad. But otherwise, a dull ache that tends to go away if I take something."

"I'd like you to start tracking your headaches, Mr. Witt. Write down when you get them, how long they last, and how bad they are on a scale of one to ten with ten being worst. Can you do that until our next appointment?"

"Yeah," I say, wondering if the headaches are a sign of something worse. I don't want to worry too much in front of the doc, though, lest he prescribe something I don't want.

The doc continues, "You said before that you've had trouble sleeping. How much sleep are you getting per night?"

"I dunno, maybe four or five hours."

"What's keeping you awake?"

"Back pain, stress of needing to get the book done, and, of course, Kayla."

He nods. "On a scale of one to ten, what would you rate your stress level?"

"I dunno," I say again, trying to think what he wants to hear. What might get me the least amount of interference or follow-up visits. But at the same time, stress might be the thing to keep him from cutting my pills. "Can stress cause hallucinations?"

"Yes, there's tons of things that can cause hallucinations; stress and lack of sleep are definitely on the list, along with other things such as mental illness."

I don't like the sound of *that*, so I say, "I'd say my stress is around a nine." This isn't far from the truth on some days, as Meg can attest to. I know I haven't been easy to live with this past year.

"Have you talked to Dr. Lavender about your stress or the hallucinations?"

"Not really," I say. "They've only come up recently. I was doing OK … or at least I *thought* I was."

"OK," Dr. Merrill says. "I'm going to prescribe a mild mood stabilizer for you. Also, a new pain medication. I'd like you to stop taking your current prescription right away, and to keep track of your mood and sleeping habits over the next few days. Also, I'd like to schedule a follow-up with you next Thursday. And I'd like you to make an appointment with Dr. Lavender if you don't already have one. OK?"

"Sounds good," I say, wanting to argue about the change in pain pills, but not wanting to get flagged as an addict. Best not to argue. If the new pills don't help, I'll just ask to go back on the old ones.

"And please," Dr. Merrill says, "get some sleep, Mr. Witt."

"Yes, sir," I say, as if it were that simple.

I'm on my way home when Meg calls. I tap the steering wheel to take the call hands-free. "Hello?"

"Hi, just checking to see how your appointment went."

"Bad news," I say, giving a dramatic pause.

"What is it?" she says, worried.

"Doc says that the MRI scan shows that I don't have a brain." I break into a laugh.

"You asshole! That's not funny!"

"Sorry," I say. "I couldn't help myself."

"So, what *did* he say?"

"He said it's probably stress and a lack of sleep. Nothing to worry about. He gave me some new meds including ... get this ... a mood stabilizer."

"Will it do anything about your being an asshole?" she jokes.

"Afraid that modern medicine has yet to find a cure for that."

She laughs. It's good to hear it. I used to make Meg laugh a lot before our lives went to hell. These small moments give me hope that maybe we can find our way back to some sense of normalcy.

"You mind if I go visit Mal?"

"Tonight?"

"Yeah, do you need me here?"

"Well," I say, suddenly not wanting her to leave me alone, but not entirely sure why. "I need to get that pitch ready for Marty."

"Already taken care of."

"What?"

"Yup, I decided that you're busy writing Book Three, and I didn't want to ruin your rhythm, so I went ahead and did it. He sent it to Johnny K to spice up, and he'll send it back to us for a look before he meets with Russell."

"Wow," I say. "Thank you!"

"You're welcome. You know you can ask me for help anytime. If you get stuck, just ask. About the book, or anything. We're partners, Tom. You don't need to go it alone."

Tears start to well up in my eyes. If she were here, I'd give her a big hug. But she's not, so I simply say, "Thank you, Meg. That's sweet of you."

"I know, I'm awesome," she says with a laugh. "OK,

I'm going to head out now unless you want me to wait for you."

Ahead of me, about a half block away, I see a dark-red pickup truck approaching a bright-red light without the slightest indication of slowing. Ahead of the truck, sitting in the middle of the same lane, is a man on a motorcycle.

The truck slams into the biker, sending him flying high into the air.

I gasp in horror as the truck then veers off the road and straight into a light pole, where it comes to a sudden stop, wrapping itself around the pole. The biker finishes his airborne takeoff, then falls to the ground, where he's hit by a blue car.

Horns and chaos erupt ahead as I slam on my brakes.

"Tom?" Meg says. "You OK?"

"Just a fender bender ahead," I lie.

She sighs, as she knows what's coming next, or perhaps has figured out the severity of the accident from my tone. "OK, I'll see you tomorrow night then."

"OK," I say, now barely aware that she's even on the phone. "Love you."

I hang up and head toward the accident.

I PULL over on the side of the street into a gas station's parking lot and get out of the car, watching as other people stop in the middle of the road, get out, and go toward the man who'd been on the motorcycle.

He's not moving.

People are on their cell phones, calling 911. Some are crying, while others rush to the man who wrapped his truck around the utility pole. I bring the camera up, zooming in and snapping shots of the chaos.

I focus on the motorcycle driver's mangled body. I can't see his face, but his arms and legs are unnaturally twisted as blood pools around him. There's no way he survived.

I turn the camera toward the red, wrinkled metal, and the careless asshole who killed the biker.

I'm shocked to see him climb out of the crumpled truck.

He's a scruffy-looking guy, mid thirties, curly brown hair. He looks wasted. I snap shots of him as he looks around. It's hard to tell if he's messed up on booze or drugs or if he's in a state of shock.

Odd that no one's approaching the scruffy man, everyone still hanging around his truck as if there's something in there worth staring at. I wonder if there was a passenger. Hard to tell from my angle.

I consider going closer, but then I see him: the man in black.

I stop, heart frozen as I stare through the lens. I snap photos, as many as I can, afraid to move the camera from my eyes lest I lose him. I continue watching as the man walks from the side of the road and toward the motorcycle driver. He looks down at him, kneels and seems to be saying something, then stands back up.

I want to pull the camera away, to see the man with my own eyes, run toward him so I can ask who he is, what the hell he's doing at these crash sites, and if he knows anything about the things I saw at the auditorium. Everything feels so connected.

But I don't dare take the camera's viewfinder from my eyes. I know if I do, he'll disappear in a blink.

I keep watching, snapping photos as the man walks away from the body and toward the dazed or drunk truck driver.

The driver sees the man in black approaching and says

something that I'm too far away to hear. The driver points back toward the remains of his truck.

The man in black nods, then puts a hand on the man's shoulder as if to reassure him that yes, he's OK.

And then, just like that, they're gone together.

I pull the camera away and scan the crowd.

I don't see either the man in black or the truck driver.

*What the hell?*

I can't stand here any longer. I rush toward the crash scene as sirens approach from not too far away.

I run past the motorcycle driver and toward the crumpled pickup truck where a crowd is gathered, still staring inside.

*What the hell are they looking at?*

An ambulance pulls up, and paramedics hop out, two rushing toward the motorcycle driver. Another two going toward the pickup. As the paramedics approach the truck's driver-side door, the crowd disperses and I finally see what they were looking at.

It's the scruffy man, crushed in the cabin, steering wheel pressing into his chest, bloody head leaning limp over the wheel, eyes staring out dead to the world.

*How?*

I fall back, trying to make sense of it when suddenly I realize, in that way you realize dream logic when you're in a dream, that the man who emerged from the wreck must've been the scruffy man's ghost.

Police arrive on the scene, and I make a mad dash back to the gas station before anyone sees me. I don't even look to see if Ruiz is one of the responding officers. I need to get back to my car so I can check the camera and see what I got.

I get to the car and climb inside, turning the camera on and reviewing the photos.

Except there are no photos.

At least not from this accident.

Instead, I see photos I don't remember taking, from inside my house.

*What the hell?*

I cycle through to the start of the sequence and look at the photos in the order they were taken:

One of the kitchen.

One of the living room, with Meg's Moleskine notebook sitting on the couch where she usually leaves it when she's been writing.

Another photo, this one of the main hallway.

Another one, in Kayla's room, from the doorway.

A chill runs through me as my head begins to pound.

Another photo of Kayla's room, this time lying on her bed and shooting up at the stars on the ceiling.

I did not take these photos.

*Did Meg?*

*And why use my camera?*

Confused, I continue.

Another photo in the hallway, this time focused on the door to the guest room that we never use.

Another photo, closer to the guest room.

And yet another shot, this time *in* the guest room. Except it looks different. Gone are the bed, bookshelf, and TV we have set up for guests.

The room is full of boxes, and the walls are painted a different color.

*What the hell is this?*

I click forward.

Back in the hallway.

It's nighttime now in the photos, I can tell from the flash.

Another photo, this one outside my bedroom door.

My headache is now pounding so hard it seems to be matching my racing pulse.

I pause my finger on the advance button, afraid to move forward. I don't know how, but I know that whatever comes next will terrify me.

I'm shaking, as ice runs through my blood.

I advance to the next photo.

A close-up of me, sleeping in my bed.

My heart is pounding as my finger hovers over the advance button.

Meg is playing some sort of joke, and I don't fucking like it. Another photo, even closer to my face, bright white in the flash.

*How did I sleep through this?*

I click forward.

And this time I'm looking at Meg sleeping.

I drop the camera.

*Oh God, who took these photos?*

I look down at the floorboard as if the camera might spring to life and attack me.

I reach down to get it, fingers closing around its body, wanting to see what's next, but also scared.

I push the advance button, and the screen is dark.

Another, dark.

And another.

And then ten more of nothing.

I'm back at the gallery's start.

I stare at the camera, trying to figure out who the hell could've done this, and more importantly, why.

Then, a knock on my window.

I turn.

# Chapter Ten

IN THE DREAM, I'm walking through a series of big iron doors groaning on oversized hinges as I push them open. As I go through each one, I feel like I'm one door deeper into the bowels of hell. The world around me is boiling hot, and as I pass through each successive door, it grows hotter.

Yet I can't stop.

I feel like I'm close to stepping through the door that harbors my memories prior to the crash.

I reach the last door. It looks vaguely familiar, not an iron door like the others, more like a door in my house.

I reach out to touch it, but its handle burns the worst.

I pull my hand back, and look down to see it boiling.

I WAKE IN THE DARK, body soaked in sweat, heart pounding as I look around, wondering first where I am, then once I realize I'm in my bedroom, how in the hell I managed to get here?

I look down, Meg is sleeping.

It's 4:12 a.m.

*I thought she was going to her sister's for the night.*

I reach to the nightstand and grab my cell phone, turn it on, and see that it's five days later.

Another chill as I try to make sense of this.

The last thing I remember is being in the car and a knock at the window. No memory of who was knocking, though.

*How can I be missing five entire days?*

I remember the photos.

I climb carefully out of bed so as not to wake Meg. Or Gus, who is sleeping in his dog bed, which is now on the floor on Meg's side. I make my way out into the hall, then up the stairs into my office.

I flick on the light and see the camera sitting on my desk in its usual spot. I pick it up and turn it on to scroll through the photos. Except the memory card is blank.

I turn on the computer, searching my photo folders, but don't see anything uploaded within the past five days.

*Did I delete them?*

I check to see the most recently updated files on my computer, and see nothing save for the Scrivener file marked, *Dark Family Book Three*, updated earlier tonight.

I open it and am surprised to see that somehow I've written seven chapters in the past five days — seven chapters I have no memory of writing.

A gnawing stirs in my gut as I remember seeing the words I'd written in a fugue state before, *Daddy, I'm not dead* over and over. If I click on a chapter and see that, I'll scream.

I hesitate, then click, and am again surprised to see actual story filling the pages.

*Did I write this?*

I read through, seeing that not only is this rough draft

good, but I'd somehow figured out a few things I'd been stuck on, chief among them how one of the main characters, Raven, could come back from what had been a certain death in the end of the last book. Of course she wasn't really dead — it was Lucina, working her dark magick to trick the family.

I have no memory at all of figuring this out.

I keep reading, waiting for something in the text to seem familiar, but none of it does. I wonder if Meg came up here and wrote this.

She wouldn't do that, would she?

No, it doesn't seem like her writing. For one, there are plenty of my usual *Tomisms*, words I typically overuse in rough drafts (*wouldn't of* instead of *wouldn't have*), words that Meg usually catches and culls. This is definitely my writing.

But how can I not remember anything from the past few days?

For the first time, I'm truly worried that this has gone beyond a minor problem. It might be something I should discuss with Dr. Merrill. But if I do that, if I tell *anyone* how bad it's gotten, Meg will freak out. She'll demand more tests we can't possibly afford. And there's no way in hell she'll let me go anywhere without her, which of course means I can't go out and shoot accident scenes.

I don't know what to do.

I suppose I should see what happens in the morning, see if she says anything like I haven't seemed myself the past few days.

I return to bed, thinking there's no way I'm ever getting back to sleep.

❧

I WAKE to the smell of blueberry muffins.

I turn and look at the clock on my nightstand: 8:11 a.m.

I get out of bed and head downstairs to find Meg sitting at the kitchen nook table, looking at Pinterest on her iPad.

"Good morning," she says, meeting my eyes with a mischievous smile.

"Um, good morning," I say, wondering why she's smiling like that. "You made muffins."

"Yes," she says. "They're still warm."

She pushes a plate and a softened butter dish and knife toward me.

I smear some butter on the muffin and take a bite, inhaling the scent of fresh-baked goodness along the way. I wonder what the occasion is.

"Last night was good," she says in a way that can only mean we had great sex. Great sex I don't remember.

I wonder if it's her fertile time, and that's why she seems especially happy. It doesn't seem like it's been a month since I missed our last good baby-making window. But hell if I can remember anything, apparently.

"Yes," I say, "almost as good as these muffins."

"Smart ass," she says, dipping her fingers in her glass of ice water and flicking drops at me.

I smile. It's great to see her in a good mood. Funny, I manage to please my wife and write seven solid chapters of our book and can't remember a single bit. I wonder if I was on some kind of autopilot, or if that me from the past five days also had no memory following the knock on the car window.

What if I wake again tomorrow with no memory of now?

I remember the months following rehab and feeling

like my body was my enemy, refusing to cooperate as I attempted to walk and learned to talk again. I don't remember the worst of it, but Meg had said when I first came out of the coma, I was in bad shape. The doctor was afraid I might never regain full consciousness.

But I was one of the lucky ones, and rebounded quickly.

From what I *do* recall, it was frustrating. I remember bits of Meg talking to me in the hospital bed, of her trying to get me to respond. I remember thinking I was talking back to her, but that she couldn't understand me. I felt like I was trapped in someone else's body, trying but unable to reach her.

This, not being able to trust my own memory, is even scarier.

I need to document this.

I decide that I'll write a message to myself on the computer, just in case I wake up tomorrow or the next day with more missing memories. I'll write in the journal each day. Perhaps that will help — assuming I remember to look.

And then I wonder: *Have I already written myself a note?*

The only places I checked for recent activity were my photo folders and my story folder. But it's possible that I wrote something in my seldom-used journal app.

I want to get up and look, but Meg starts talking.

"How's the writing?"

"I got seven chapters done," I say, hoping I hadn't already told her that yesterday morning.

"Great! I figured you were making progress, considering how quiet you were the past few days, and how you barely left the office … well, until last night, anyway."

She smiles like a minx, and I wish I remember what we

did. I can't recall ever earning *that kind* of response, even on a great night.

A terrifying thought enters my head — *split personality*. I developed schizophrenia, and my alter ego isn't just a great writer but also a great lover!

I wonder if it's possible. Perhaps it's one of those things that Dr. Merrill was saying could be behind the hallucinations. I want to ask him when I go back, but how do I bring it up without inviting myself for even more exams and medications?

I stuff the rest of the muffin in my mouth, trying to conjure the words for an exit.

"Well, I should get back to work," I say, waiting to see her reaction.

"OK, just don't forget about tonight."

*Shit. What's tonight?*

I smile, as if joking just in case tonight is something super important, "Remind me again?"

"You're taking me to the grief meeting with you, remember? We talked about getting through this together."

I hope my first emotion, sheer terror, doesn't show through as I say, "Oh yeah, of course."

Meg looks at me suspiciously, "Unless you don't *want me* to go with you?"

*No, of course I don't want you to go with me. I don't want to go! I don't want to see Sam or those damned things, whatever they were.*

But I can't tell her that. And considering how well things seem to be going between us this morning, I don't want to risk ruining it. Whatever I did the past few days, I must've been on my best behavior.

"Of course we'll go," I say, "but I better get some work done first."

"Do you want me to go over anything you've written yet?"

I'm not sure why she'd ask this, as I typically don't hand her anything until I'm finished with my first or second draft. Had I promised to share earlier? Or is she just trying to ease the burden of writing this first draft under a deadline?

"No, not yet," I say. "But thank you."

I get up, take my plate to the sink, then come back and kiss her. "Off to work."

"Love you."

"I love you," I say, eager to get upstairs and see what messages I may have left for myself.

I OPEN the journal app and see that I did leave recent updates!

*SATURDAY*

*"Meg and I had a huge fight after she came home earlier and found me passed out in the car, covered in vomit.*

*I can't remember what happened. Last thing I remember is seeing the man on the motorcycle get hit. Everything's blank after that.*

*That's why I'm writing in here. To try and keep track of stuff.*

*I have trouble remembering too many things lately. From my writing, to things I did just a few days ago. For instance, the grief meeting. I know something happened there, but it's a blur.*

*I need to go back."*

*WEIRD.*

I remember the grief meeting, but don't remember writing this.

*How is that possible?*

I consider the schizoid thing again. Could I have developed a part of me who remembers some, but not all, things?

I keep reading.

*"SUNDAY*

*Meg and I fought again.*

*I admitted that I needed help. I told her that I was having problems remembering stuff. She called the doctor, on the weekend no less, and told him, even though I didn't want her to.*

*She also moved my appointment from Friday to tomorrow.*

*I've decided not to fight it.*

*Truth is, I don't feel myself. I'm hyperemotional, crying every time I think of Kayla or pass by her bedroom. I thought it would be easier after a while. They say time heals all wounds, right?*

*Mine only deepen.*

*I need to channel my pain, put it to use.*

*I'm going to buckle down and work on the story, pouring these feelings into it."*

So I HAD an appointment I can't even remember?

I read on, eager to find out what happened at the appointment. I hope he didn't change my pain meds.

I open my desk and see two bottles, one of the old pills, and another bottle of the new ones.

OK, we're good for now.

I read on.

*"MONDAY*

*Dr. Lavender and Dr. Merrill came to the house together.*

*I didn't know doctors made house calls, let alone together. It felt like some kind of intervention.*

*Meg made me fess up.*

*I told them about the accident, then waking up covered in vomit in the driveway.*

*They asked me about the man in black, if I'd seen him again.*

*I had no idea what they were talking about.*

*Meg reminded me that I said I'd seen a man in black while out taking pictures of crashes, and that when I went to show Officer Ruiz, he wasn't in the photos. Apparently, I made a big deal about this, but can't remember a thing.*

*Everyone looked at me, worried.*

*Meg was practically in tears asking what was wrong with me, if I might slip back into a coma.*

*Dr. Merrill says no, but there may be damage they've not yet picked up on.*

*Dr. Lavender went on this whole thing about how there's so much we don't understand about our own brains. That our minds are puzzle-solving machines, and that perhaps mine is taking bits of missing information and trying to put a puzzle together where there is none, creating this man in black because some part of me needs it to make sense of things.*

*He says that sometimes people with traumatic brain injuries have lingering issues that take years, if not a lifetime, to recover from. This could be that, or it could be as simple as adjusting my meds.*

*The shrink says he would like to see me twice a week starting next week. He can make house calls for one of the visits, but for the other, I'll need to go see him.*

*After they left, Meg seemed both relieved and scared. Relieved that I'm not going to slip back into a coma, but scared that something's still wrong that we may not be able to get right.*

*After the "intervention," I went back to the office to write."*

. . .

IF ONLY THE doctors knew that the ME they were talking to is one I don't remember being!

*"TUESDAY MORNING*

*I saw her!*

*I saw Kayla.*

*I was writing late at night. It was 4:01 a.m., I remember looking at the clock and thinking I ought to get to bed. Then I looked out the window, out at the graveyard, and saw a girl standing there, looking up at my window.*

*I ran downstairs as fast as I could and raced over to the church, but by the time I got there, she was gone.*

*I know it was her, though.*

*No child would be standing out in a graveyard at this hour.*

*I want to tell Meg, but know I should keep it to myself.*

*For now."*

THAT IS THE LAST ENTRY, dated the day before I remember waking up.

I wonder if I truly saw her. Or, if like Dr. Lavender said, it's my mind creating fictions in an attempt to solve some sort of puzzle.

If so, what puzzle?

I'm trying to remember the missing months of my life leading up to the accident. Trying to remember the accident itself. Why wouldn't my mind create backstories to fill that void? Maybe give me memories of a nice tropical vacation with my wife and daughter? Something useful. Not men in black, ghosts, and all this other nonsense.

*Because you've become a hack horror writer, and this is what you get.*

I laugh at my inner critic, wishing it were as simple as

that. But this doesn't feel like some puzzle I'm creating for myself. Or even a reaction to medication or a result of my brain injury. There's something else going on. It feels real. As real as the desk I'm sitting at. The journal I'm staring at rather than writing the book I should be writing.

Something is happening.

And tonight, I plan to figure it out.

I'll go to the grief meeting. And if I see ghosts, maybe Meg will, too.

Or she'll have me committed.

# Chapter Eleven

We're in the auditorium, sitting toward the back where I was before.

I'm wearing my black Yankees hat even though Meg thinks I look ridiculous, that it calls even more attention to myself. She said I look like I'm sneaking into a porno theater or something.

The Together Through Grief meeting starts the same as the last, with Marcy Harris kicking things off with an introduction.

As she's talking, I look around, searching for signs of Sam, or anything else that should not be.

But everything seems normal, just like it *feels*.

I can't explain it well, but I had this sensation during the last meeting, like something didn't feel real. I don't know if I sensed it while everything was happening, or not until later, when thinking about it, but there was this almost dreamlike quality, like if I touched any of the walls or people within it, they would melt away to something else.

I know I was at the meeting, of that I have no doubt. I know I spoke with Kathy.

But the stuff with Sam, and what happened after — that felt somehow outside of reality. Like a hallucination.

Being here in this stiff chair, surrounded by people, sitting next to Meg, and hearing mourners as they shuffle into the room, taking seats closer to us, everything feels more real.

Marcy is followed by a man and woman talking about losing their son, an infant, in his sleep. As they're talking, Meg's hand finds mine in the darkness, and squeezes it.

I look at her, and she's staring at the stage, transfixed, tears welling in her eyes.

I wonder if this meeting's stated purpose, getting through grief, is as much for her as it is for me.

She lost a daughter, too.

And then I start to wonder if maybe I've been wrong all along. Here I thought she was holding things together so well, but perhaps she simply did a better job of pretending things were OK than I did. She never had time to grieve, to tend to her mental wounds, as she was suddenly expected to be strong enough to help me in my physical recovery. She had to be strong, for both of us.

I feel suddenly selfish and horrible to have been wallowing in my misery, out all night chasing ghosts and trying to remember, when what I *should* have been doing is focusing on Meg, trying to be the anchor she needs — that our family needs — to start anew.

I squeeze her hand tighter, so damned glad to have her in my life.

I feel tears welling in my own eyes.

I decide that I need to kick these pain pills.

I'll go see the doctors and tell them everything — from

the blackouts to the missing memories to the ghosts to seeing Kayla. Everything.

After three more people, Marcy asks, "Who would like to share next?"

Meg asks, "Did you go up?"

"What?" I whisper, "me?"

"Yeah, did you go up last time?"

"No," I say, shaking my head. "I can't."

"Want me to go with you?"

"No," I say, meeting her eyes, hoping she won't try and force me. I'm ready to do a lot of things, but going up on stage? Not gonna happen.

She asks, "Would you mind if I went up?"

I'm surprised, and sure my face shows it. I stammer a bit before saying, "No, not at all, if you want to."

"I do," she says, then stands and heads toward the stage.

I shift uncomfortably in my chair as people look at her, then me. I wonder how many of them know who we are. Kathy, sitting three rows ahead, looks back and gives me a little wave. I nod, then wave back, sinking lower into my seat.

Meg, now on stage and at the mic, says, "Hi, my name is Meg, and my husband and I lost our child last year."

As she starts, I feel a gnashing in my gut over the uncertainty of what she might say. We've always been private people — especially following the accident. It took us months to agree to publicity again, and even then, it was under our terms. The *Entertainment Weekly* interview was about as much as we've talked about Kayla, and even that was uncomfortable.

To think that Meg is about to put it all out there to this room full of strangers makes me feel naked, exposed, and vulnerable.

She continues, "It's weird. Even after a year, I find myself thinking about Kayla, waking up and wanting to share something with her, or being in a store and wanting to buy her something I think she'll love. Then I catch myself, and remember. I think the worst was on Mother's Day. My husband, Tom, got me a Mother's Day card but wasn't sure whether I'd want it or not, whether it would serve as a reminder that I'm no longer a mom. I thought to myself, yes, I lost a daughter, but I still *feel* like a mother? Does that make sense?"

The crowd nodded, and some said "mm hmm" aloud.

I'm watching Meg and marveling at her strength to speak about this, when I notice a chill in the room, punctuated with a sharp pain in my head.

*No, not now.*

While I'd welcomed something happening, especially if Meg could be here to witness it, I find myself wanting to cling to the moment, this raw moment with Meg. I feel like I'm getting closer to something I've been missing between us, and perhaps that can do more good than any of this man in black or ghost child nonsense. I feel like a boat unmoored, lost at sea, shifting between what is real and what is not. I feel like if I can just drop an anchor in the moment, in this reality right here and now with Meg, then I can have a normal life again.

The pain in my head subsides, and I breathe a sigh of relief that perhaps I am able to control things — to keep things from spiraling out of control.

Then I hear a voice behind me.

"Why don't you go up with her?"

I turn and see Sam standing behind me.

*No, no, no.*

I try and tell myself that the ghost of Kathy's dead son

isn't here, that I'm imagining this. I turn away and don't respond, hoping he'll go away.

"Did you give my mother the message yet?" Sam asks, leaning closer, now over my shoulder. An icy chill runs through me, and I shiver.

"No," I whisper. "You're not real."

"Not real?" Sam says. "I know you can see me."

"That doesn't make you real, and the conversation is over," I say, not wanting to get into an argument with a figment of my imagination.

"Please tell her," Sam begs.

I ignore him. The more I do, though, the realer he feels. It's as if he is imposing his reality over mine, and it's pissing me off. I just want him gone. I want to be with my wife, we'll go home, make love, and then tomorrow I'll call the doctors, tell them everything, take whatever medicines they want. We'll heal, we'll get through this, and life will go on.

It's all I want. No more trying to remember the accident and what came before. No more going out and taking pictures of horrible crash sites.

*Just let me have this, God, please.*

"Please," he says, voice louder, getting angry, "tell her!"

The auditorium lights flicker above us.

I remember how his anger had preceded the arrival of those things last time, and wonder if perhaps I should give in. If he, and those things, *are* real, and they can sense that I see them, might I be in danger? Might I endanger Meg and everyone in here?

I need to short circuit his anger, which means I need to take control of the situation and acknowledge his reality.

"I can't tell her here. Let me find a time when there's not so many people around."

"How do I know you will?"

"You don't," I say. "But if I'm going to do it, it has to be on my terms, not yours."

"Why are you being so mean?"

"I'm not being mean, I'm being honest. I need to find your mom in the right mood, to be receptive to something as insane as this will sound. If I tell her now, she won't believe me. Hell, *I* barely believe me. For all I know, you're something I made in my head."

He's quiet, as if mulling over my words.

He then says, "You didn't tell your wife about me?"

"Good God, no. She's already worried about my sanity."

"What if I can prove I'm real, to both of you?"

"What do you mean?"

"I've seen your daughter."

I turn to him, stare into his brown eyes. "What?"

"Kayla, right?"

"Where did you see her?"

"She's here, right now." The boy pointed. "Right next to you."

I look around, but see no sign of my daughter. Chills run across my flesh as desperation fills my gut.

"Where is she?"

"She's right here," Sam says, still pointing to the spot beside my chair.

I look, but see nothing. I reach out as if I might feel something. "Why can't I see her?" I ask, wondering if Sam's lying to me, and hoping he isn't.

"I don't know," he says. "I still don't even know why *you* can see me. You're the only living person who has seen me so far."

"What did you mean you can prove you're real?" I ask.

Sam says, "Ask me something only Kayla will know."

I try to think of something, but as I'm thinking I hear

applause and see Meg leaving the stage. My heart is pounding fast as I try to think of something before she gets back. I can't have this conversation in front of her — *can I?*

But if Sam is real, and I'm *not* losing my mind, I need to prove it to her. Perhaps Sam *can* prove it to us both.

I move aside so that Meg can sit.

Behind me, Sam says, "Ask me something only Kayla would know."

A couple of minutes ago, I was ready to come clean, tell Meg — and the doctors — everything, even give up the pills if they were part of the problem. But now, with Sam whispering behind me, I can't help but follow this lead, to see if this weird shit is, in fact, reality.

"How'd I do?" Meg asks.

"You did great, honey." I lean over and kiss her on the cheek, then hold her hand and whisper. "I have to tell you something, and need you to promise me you won't freak out."

"What?" she asks nervously.

"The last time I came here I saw something."

"What?"

"Remember, no freaking out."

"What is it?" She looks at me like she's a moment away from doing the very thing I asked her not to do.

"You see that woman three rows up on the end? The one with the blue blouse?"

"Yeah," Meg says, brow furrowed as she's wondering where I'm going.

"Her son, Sam, died a few months ago. And … " *here we go*, "I saw him. Here. Last week."

She looks at me and grins uncomfortably. "Shut up."

"No, I'm serious."

"You *saw* him? *Here?* You're telling me you saw a ghost, Tom?"

She pulls her hand away, crossing her arms over her chest as she tends do when she's unhappy with me. I feel like I'm testing the limits of her patience. If Sam falls through, I'm fucked with a capital F. Meg will think I'm batshit crazy.

"Yes, and there's one other thing."

She looks at me, "What?"

"He's behind us right now."

Meg looks back, then at me. She laughs, "You're messing with me, right?"

The way she was looking at me a second ago, scared, juxtaposed against the smile now in her eyes as she laughs, makes me want to say that yes, I am messing with her. Big joke, ha ha, let's go home and forget all about this. Maybe get ice cream, settle down, watch some Netflix, and call it a night.

Sam, seeming to sense my hesitancy, says, "Tell her, Mr. Tom."

The lights flicker above. I wonder if Meg even notices.

"There's more."

She doesn't want to hear more, though. Her lips purse as she barely manages to get out a "What?"

"Kayla is here, too."

She starts to stand, but I put my hand down firm on her leg and press down, more forceful than I've ever touched her, to keep Meg in her seat.

She looks at me with fire in her eyes. "This isn't funny, Tom."

I swallow, "I'm not joking, Meg. I can't see Kayla, but Sam says she's here, right next to us, and he *can* see her. I didn't believe him at first, either," I say like I've already convinced her that Sam is here. "He said to ask him a question only Kayla would know, so that he can prove it to me. Prove it to us."

Meg shakes her head, looking like she's on the verge of tears. "I'm not doing this, Tom."

"What?"

"I'm not contributing to whatever … whatever's wrong with you. I love you, Tom. You know that, but I can't do this. You need help."

She gets up, her seat bouncing loudly, and brushes by me, walking fast toward the exit. I can feel the eyes of others on me, even though I don't dare meet them.

I hop out of my seat and follow her out of the auditorium — into the hallway where those things chased me from the school.

Sam is following close behind me, not saying a word. I hope that Kayla is also following, and if she is, that she isn't too upset by seeing her mother react this way.

"Meg!" I say once the doors close behind me and before she can head out into the parking lot, "Wait!"

She stops and turns, no longer able to keep her tears from flooding, staring at me as I run up to her. I know she doesn't want hear any more crazy talk, but some part of her, thank God, makes her wait to see what I'll say.

"I didn't want to tell you any of this, Meg. I thought I might be going crazy, too. And hell, maybe I am. If so, this is a chance to prove it, right? Ask Sam something that only you and Kayla would know. Some mother daughter secret I never knew. I'm sure there's gotta be something."

She looks at me like I've totally lost it. "Ask Sam? I don't *see* Sam, Tom! And neither do you."

"Just think of something!" I snap, pissed that she won't take a chance. "If I'm wrong, I'll never bring it up again! I'll go to whatever doctor you want, but just fucking ask *something!*"

Outside of the bedroom, I never speak roughly to Meg.

105

She looks at me, startled. Her eyes wander up to the ceiling, as if she's considering my offer.

"Something that only Kayla and I know?"

"Yes," I say. I turn to Sam and ask, "Is she here? Is Kayla here?"

Sam looks a few feet behind him, then back at me. He nods. "Yes, but she's crying."

I turn back to Meg, "Anything … please."

"OK," Meg says, "what was the name of the porcupine she asked me to write a story about?"

She folds her arms as she stares at me, waiting.

I turn to Sam. "Did you hear that?"

"Yes," he says, then turns to ask the space behind him, where I still can't believe that Kayla is standing.

Sam is quiet.

"Did she say anything?" I ask.

Meg sighs, like she can't believe she's entertaining my delusions.

Sam says, "Try" to the space behind him.

He looks at me. "She can't remember."

I feel punched in the gut.

Meg, more impatient: "Well?"

Sam says, "Ask her something else."

I swallow the lump in my throat, not wanting to prolong this torture. I look at Meg, who is staring at me with something I can only describe as hate — if she were capable of hating me. I say, "She can't remember. Ask something else."

Meg spins on her heel and heads straight to the doors.

"Meg!" I call out in vain.

She ignores me, heading toward the car.

I turn to Sam and shake my head, pissed at him because I can't be pissed at a daughter who isn't here. "Thanks a lot!"

"Kayla says she's sorry!"

I want to believe him. More than anything.

I decide to give him one more chance, but have to be quick because I have the keys to the car and Meg won't wait. She'd sooner walk the four miles home than wait for me when she's this angry.

"OK," I say to Sam, "one question. From me."

"OK," Sam says, eyes hopeful. "Shoot."

"What's Kayla's middle name?"

"Her middle name?"

"Yeah, that's so easy that *you* could probably even guess it, Sam," I say, almost accusing him of lying just to get me to deliver the message to his mother.

Sam turns and asks the space behind him. He looks nervous.

"Come on," I say, "I need to go get my wife."

He turns, frowning, "She say's she can't remember."

I look at Sam and let out a deep sigh. "Bullshit."

"I swear, Mr. Tom! Kayla's upset. She can't remember!"

I shake my head. "Stop it. Stop it. You're not real."

I turn and head toward the doors.

"Yes, I am!" Sam yells. The lights flicker, as if in response. But I'm not buying it.

No more.

"No, you're not!" I yell back as I push through the doors and out into the parking lot. It's dark and has started to rain. I see Meg approaching the main gate. *She's actually going to walk home in the rain!*

I chase after her, cold rain like ice on my skin, calling out, but she ignores me.

I get in the car, soaking the seat, and stick my keys in the ignition, hoping she doesn't try to lose me in the neighborhood streets off the main road. Meg is the world's nicest person, but when she feels you've taken advantage of her, she's like a cornered animal.

I turn on the car, throw it into reverse, pull out of the parking space, click on my lights, and press down on the gas, fishtailing as I race toward the exit.

I reach her just as she's turning out of the parking lot and onto the sidewalk. I pull up in the grass beside her. Thunder rumbles overhead as I roll down the window.

"Get in!" I shout over the now-howling wind.

"No!" she says, still walking.

"Come on, Meg, it's pouring!" I say, pulling up a bit.

"No! I'll walk," she cries out as lightning crashes above. As the light brightens her face for a moment, her eyes seem like they're almost glowing in a beautiful haunted blue.

"Come on, you'll get hit by lightning!" I argue.

"I can't do this anymore, Tom!" she yells as thunder explodes in the heavens.

I don't know what she means by "this."

*Entertain my delusions? Or … be married to me?*

I can't ask. Not now. I need to get her in the car. We can talk about this when she's safe and out of the rain.

"Just let me drive you home. Please, Meg!"

She keeps walking, ignoring my pleas.

I throw the car into park, key the ignition off, hop out, throw the door shut, and leave it there in the swale. I run up behind her.

"I'm not letting you walk home alone. If you get hit by lightning, I want to, too."

She shakes her head, refusing to look at me, keeping her pace.

The rain is cold and falling hard. We're both soaked. She in her dress and brown leather jacket, I in my jeans and navy long-sleeve button-down. Our shoes are certainly ruined.

She keeps walking, ignoring me.

"Come on," I say. "Get in the car. Hell, you can drive home without me if you want. I'll walk! But, please, I don't want you getting hit by lightning, or a shitty driver. Come on, Meg. I can't lose you, too."

She turns and looks at me, as if considering my offer. I wonder if she *would* let me walk home alone. I don't think she would, but then again, I don't think she's ever been this mad at me.

I reach into my pocket and offer her the car keys.

She meets my eyes. It's hard to tell if she's still crying, what with all the rain, but I assume that she is.

She asks, "You think I'm *mad* at you?"

I'm not sure if this is a trick question, but the way she's looking at me, I think she's being serious.

"Um, yeah?"

"I'm not mad," she says. "I'm scared, Tom. I don't know what's happening inside your head, and one minute I think you're OK, but then you go and do something like this. And I don't know what to do. I thought I could be strong enough to get you through this, but I … I don't know if I can."

"What are you saying?"

"I don't know."

Now I'm crying.

I look down, unsure what to say. I look up at Meg, meet her eyes, and feel like the woman I've loved for half of my life has given up on me. Even in the worst of times — during rehab and following the loss of Kayla — I knew that when I looked in her eyes that things would be OK because she loved me, she believed in me. That faith has faded, maybe it's gone.

I can't think of a single thing to say that might bring it back.

"How long have you felt like this?" I didn't think things were that bad. Or that I'd seemed *that* crazy. Hell, I hadn't even told her the craziest shit until now.

"I don't know. I thought we would get past this, just like the other stuff, but now …"

I want to beg for her not to give up on me. To tell her that I'll get help, that I'll see any doctor she wants. Just please don't lose hope. But some part of me won't let me ask. I don't want to be a burden. She's already sacrificed so much for us, for me, ever since Kayla died. She had to put her own grief on hold to help me heal, and I can't ask anything of her. It wouldn't be fair.

She asks, "Do you really believe our daughter was there tonight?"

I stare at her, not sure what to say, or think. If I believe that Sam was there, why wouldn't I believe that Kayla was, too? I can't think of a reason for Sam to lie.

I shrug.

"I don't know what I believe any more."

She hugs me.

We stand, embracing in the pouring rain for a long time.

Both of us crying.

As the rain starts to die down, she looks up at me, and I think for a moment that she's going to kiss me and that all is forgiven.

Instead, she says, "Let's go home."

# Chapter Twelve

I WAKE at 2:15 p.m.

My head is pounding. Beside me, on Meg's pillow, is a pink envelope.

I open it, wiping my eyes, trying to get rid of the blur. Finally, words swim into focus.

*"Staying with my sister for a few days to think about things.*

*I love you, Tom. Please get help.*

*If you need anything, call me.*

*Love,*

*Meg"*

I stare at it, thinking that this is it.

The end of our marriage.

I've heard stories, some even in the grief meetings, of marriages falling apart after the loss of a child. Nothing is ever the same. Hell, it's tough enough to stay married even in the best of situations.

People change.

Many people I went to school with who got married young are now on their second or third marriages. Rarely are we the same person we were ten or twenty years ago.

Neither are our spouses. It's almost impossible to know how these things will shake out. Will the *us* that got married still be as compatible years down the road? It takes more than love to stay together against the seas of change that want to tear us apart. It takes strength, and devotion.

I thought the worst was behind us, but I could never have predicted this.

I sit on the edge of my bed, wondering if there's any way to save my marriage.

Gus comes over to my side and lays his head on my lap, brow furrowed as his eyes look up to mine. He lets out a soft, almost sympathetic whine.

"It'll be OK, boy," I say and pet his head. His tail immediately starts thumping on the floor.

I find myself smiling, and — oddly hopeful.

Meg's right.

I need to get help.

I need to stop the pills.

Need to tell the doctor everything. Both the docs.

Twelve days later ...

6:15 p.m.

I'm waiting for my microwave dinner to finish cooking so I can head back to my office, eat a bit, and catch up on some reader emails.

It's been seven days since I've taken the pain pills.

It's been ten days since I started taking these antidepressants.

It's been eleven days since I came clean and told the shrink, Dr. Lavender, everything.

In that time, I've avoided the accidents. I haven't gone back to the grief meetings, and I've been a good boy, staying in my office and writing from dawn to dusk, then going to bed at night and actually getting good sleep, thanks to sleeping pills and the daily exercise of walking twice a day, morning and evening, for an hour each time.

I'd love to say that I feel better, but I'm still in pain, though no horrible headaches lately, and my temper is short. Fortunately, Meg's not around to suffer my mood swings.

She's still at her sister's. I told her about my progress, and she's hopeful. But she's helping Mallory through some stuff at the moment. It's tough to tell if Mal truly needs her there or if she's just not convinced that I'm really on the path to being better. I won't push it, though. Maybe this time apart will do us both some good.

I'll keep getting better and writing this damned book, while Meg does whatever it is she needs to do.

I'll have faith: This isn't the end of our marriage. We've been through too much shared history, and recently, mutual trauma, to be with anyone else.

But perhaps that's also a reason to split.

Maybe she can't look at me without thinking about all that we've lost together. Perhaps the only way to be happy is to start over, with someone else. Easier to avoid the past than have to keep living through it.

Dr. Lavender has helped me to discover that I may have been doing something similar. While Meg wasn't a constant reminder of our loss, perhaps I'd seen the process of having another child as something I couldn't bear pouring my hopes into. Perhaps that's why we've failed in our attempts. The doctor seems to think that I buried myself in the *busyness* of photographing car crashes to avoid rebuilding a family — that I was afraid to have another child and lose it. And that everything else — the man in black, the ghosts, the visions of my daughter, and those things at the school — were all my mind wanting to avoid the real issue: my fear of loss.

At first, I rejected the idea as psychobabble. But the more I thought about it, the more it made sense. More than a supernatural explanation, anyway.

Lavender says that a normal schedule with established routines will help me rebuild my life. So I'm doing my best and trying to stay focused on my work.

~

1:16 a.m.

It's hardest at night.

Harder to not take the pills.

Hard to be alone.

I'm lying in bed, my back aching, trying to sleep, watching the clock's blue numbers in the dark as the six turns to a seven.

This is the latest I've been up in nearly two weeks.

I know what will put me to sleep. I know what will calm the incessant thoughts and worries, what will ease the pain: the pain pills.

I tell myself no, but it's the same argument I've been having for the past four hours.

After a while, it becomes pointless to lie to oneself.

I know what I'm going to do even before my feet hit the carpet and carry me up the stairs to my writing room. I reach for the desk where I stashed the bottles, telling myself just this once. Only for sleep.

If everything else in my life is under control, then the pain pills can't hurt anything, right? Millions of people around the world take pain pills without incident. Yeah, some are hooked and get in a terrible way, but they don't see ghosts and hallucinate. I think the antidepressants may help keep me grounded, in reality.

I look at the bottle. My hand is shaking.

I tell myself to just put the bottle away, to go back to bed. But I can't sleep if I don't take them. And if I can't sleep, things will get really bad. I tell myself that it's in my best interest to take the pills. It wasn't like the doctor said the pills were the problem. Both doctors said they weren't an issue if well managed.

I think almost two weeks without them is well fucking managed.

I untwist the cap, take one, and swallow.

I chase it with a bottle of water on my desk and sit back in my chair, waiting for that good feeling to wash through me. Pain dulled, thoughts turned happy. It makes sleep so much easier.

I close my eyes and allow myself a smile, anticipating the coming bliss.

The pills' only negative is that nobody's yet found a way to divorce the opiates within them from the negative effects that come with relief. I researched heroin users for one of our characters in *Dark Family* and learned that they're always chasing another high as good as the first, but as with many drugs, highs are harder to come by and you need to take more and more just to feel something close. Eventually, and here's where opiates are most dangerous, you need them to feel normal.

I wonder how far down that road I am now.

I don't *think* I'm an addict. Would an addict be able to go almost two weeks without taking a pill? I doubt it. But like heroin users, I do find that the bliss never lasts as long, and on days I don't take pills I don't feel the same. My mood is worse, and I'm quicker to anger.

I continue to wait for the feeling that the pill has kicked

in. It's like the warmth of happiness, which one moment I don't feel and then the next I do.

Sometimes, it takes fifteen minutes. Other times, a half hour.

I open my eyes to see how long it's been since I swallowed the pill and scream as I see the shape in front of my desk.

Sam.

Standing between my desk and the window looking out over the graveyard.

"No," I say, shaking my head, "you are not here."

"I am here, Tom. I've been here for the past twelve days, but you haven't seen me."

No, this is not how hallucinations work. A pill doesn't make you hallucinate that quickly. *Does it?*

"I'm going to bed now." I don't know why I'm talking to my imagination. I get up, turn around, and head toward the door.

"Paige!" he calls out.

I turn back to him.

"What?"

"Your daughter's middle name is Paige."

I stare at Sam, a cold chill running through me. I can hear my heart pounding.

Of course *Sam* would know that, because *I* know her middle name.

"That doesn't prove anything."

Sam looks to his left, talking, "You sure?"

Is he talking to her?

No, I can't let myself fall for this.

I need my bed, and to put this behind me.

Sam says, "Percy."

"Percy?" I ask, "What are you talking about?"

"The other question you asked Kayla. The porcupine's name. It was Percy."

He then says, "She's next to me, too, Tom. Kayla is here."

I stare, not at Sam, but at the space beside him.

*Is she really here?*

Sam asks, "Well? Is it Percy?"

"I don't know. Meg didn't tell me."

"Come on, Mr. Tom, you have to believe me."

"Wait a second," I say. "I'll be right back."

I click on my computer and locate the network drive that Meg and I share.

I type in *Percy* and wait to see if anything comes up of a story she's working on.

Nothing shows.

I look down at my cell phone, which I'd left on my desk earlier rather than taking it to bed.

I pick it up, find Meg's name, and dial.

It's 1:27 a.m.

I'm sure she's sleeping, and even more certain she'll be pissed. But what else am I going to do? She already hates me, already thinks I'm mental. The worse I can do is ruin the hope nursed through the past twelve days and go back to start — I hope that's as bad as it can get.

"'Ello?" she says, groggy.

"Hey, Meg, I have to ask you something."

"Are you OK?" she asks, suddenly alert. "Did you black out again?"

"No, Meg, I just need to ask you something. If I'm wrong, just please hang up, and we can talk about it next time, or not."

"What is it?" she asks, her voice laced with accusation that I've been taking pills, or gone off the ones I'm supposed to be taking.

"Percy," I say. "Was that the name of the porcupine?"

She's quiet on the other end. I think she's crying.

"Is that it?" I ask again.

"I'm not doing this again, Tom. Please, just go to sleep."

"Just answer the question!" I snap.

"Yes, his name was Percy."

I turn, staring at Sam, and the space next to him. I see something, just slightly shifting. A shimmer in the air, a blur, which just as quickly vanishes.

I swallow, tears streaming down my cheeks.

"Kayla?" I ask.

"What are you talking about, Tom?" Meg says in the phone, either scared or pissed, or more likely, both.

"She's here," I say. "She just told me Percy."

"No, Tom, She's not there. You probably heard her talking about it, and you just remembered it in a dream or something."

"Ask me something else that only she would know."

"Stop it, Tom!" she says. She's definitely crying.

"Please," I say, not disguising my tears, "just ask."

"I can't," she says, and hangs up.

I stare at the phone, enraged.

*How can she hang up now? When I can prove that I'm not crazy, that Kayla is here?*

I hit redial and call, but it goes straight to voicemail.

"Dammit, Meg, pick up. Just one more question, something I won't know. *Please*."

I hang up and put the phone on the desk, certain that she won't call back.

I turn back to Sam.

"She's here, right now?"

"Yes, she's standing right in front of you."

I fall to my knees. "Kayla?" I'm not sure what I expect. Perhaps some warm touch, or maybe a cold one. An embrace. Her voice. I'd heard Kayla before, calling me in my sleep, unless *that* was a hallucination. Maybe she can reach me now.

Sam asks, "Can you hear her?"

"No," I say, crying.

"She says that she loves you. She's also hugging you."

"I can't feel it, honey," I say, wiping tears from my face. "I can't feel you or hear you."

"I miss you so much, baby. Oh God, I wish you were here."

"She says she misses you and Mommy, too. She says that she's sorry that Mommy doesn't believe you. She knows that Mommy wants to, but can't."

I nod my head yes. "Your mommy misses you every day," I say, wishing I could look into her eyes. I ask, "Where are you? I mean when you're not here? Are you in heaven?"

Sam says, "She can't go to heaven."

I look up at him, feeling like he just hit me in the face with a shovel. "What?"

"We can't move on until we let go."

"What do you mean?" I ask.

"The man in black told me that we can't move on until we let go."

"You saw him? The man in black? He's real?"

"Yes, I saw him after the last time you came to the auditorium. He was helping the old man across the street to move on."

"What do you mean? What is he?"

"He helps us move on after we die. Some of us are ready to go to wherever we're supposed to go, but some of us have what he called 'unfinished business.' Like with me.

SEAN PLATT & DAVID W WRIGHT

Before I can move on, I need to let my mom know it wasn't her fault, that I wasn't really trying to kill myself."

"What's Kayla's unfinished business?" I ask, unable to imagine something preventing her from moving on. It's not like Sam's situation. She died in a car accident, not due to an accidental overdose or something. What unfinished business could she have?

Sam says, "I'm sorry, Kayla, but I can't tell him. Not until he helps me."

"Damn it, Sam!" I yell. "Tell me what she said."

"I'm sorry, Mr. Tom, but first I need you to give my mom the message."

"Fine," I say. "Should I call her now?"

"No," Sam says, "go to our house."

"Now? In the middle of the night?"

"She's still up," he says. "I was just there."

"I tell her, and then you'll help Kayla?"

"Yes," he says. "And in turn, it will help your family."

# Chapter Thirteen

I DRIVE to Kathy's house alone. Apparently ghosts can't ride in a car. But using the address Sam gave me, along with my phone's turn-by-turn navigation, I find it easily, a quarter mile from my own home.

I pull up. All the windows of the house are dark save for one on the second story, light bleeding through a gauzy white curtain.

I park on the street, along with the other cars lining the quiet suburban block of homes built in the fifties and sixties. It's an older neighborhood, but even this late at night, I can see that the homes are well taken care of.

I get out of the car and see Sam standing in front of the house, eagerly waiting. He looks happy to see me, but also nervous. Does he think his mom won't believe me? Or perhaps those things will show up and take him away?

"Thank you," he says.

"I'm gonna tell her, but I can't promise she'll believe me. Either way, you're going to tell me what Kayla said. You got it?"

"Yes, sir."

I ring the doorbell.

While I wait on the doorstep, wondering if she'll even acknowledge I'm here as I sure as hell wouldn't answer the door in the middle of the night myself, I look at Sam, pacing back and forth nervously.

I ask if Kayla is here.

Sam says no, that she's back at my house, waiting.

After a couple of minutes, I ring the bell again. Now I'm growing nervous.

The porch light comes on, and the curtain in the window beside the door is pulled back to reveal Kathy's widening eyes.

"Mr. Witt?" she asks from the other side of the window.

"Yes, Mrs. Prescott, I need to talk to you."

The curtain falls back into place, and a moment later the door locks tumble open.

She opens the door and looks me up and down. "Are you OK?"

"Yes," I say. "I know it's late, and I apologize, but I need to talk to you about Sam. May I come in?"

"Sam?" she asks, confused. "Yes," she says, opening the door and letting me in.

Sam follows me inside.

Kathy leads me to the dining room in the rear of the house, and flicks on a light. "Can I get you a drink?"

"No," I say as I take a seat, "thank you."

She sits down across from me, pulling her blue robe closed over a pink shirt. "You wanted to talk about Sam?"

I wonder what she thinks I want to discuss. Maybe she thinks I want to talk to her for a story I'm doing, even though it would be incredibly rude to be here at *this* hour for something like an interview. Whatever she thinks, nothing will prepare her for the truth. And even as I'm about to deliver it, I can feel Sam's eyes on me and his mother, watching, waiting.

As I look into Kathy's eyes — the eyes of a pragmatic, sad woman — I wonder how the hell am I supposed to convince her of something I couldn't even convince my wife?

I hope Sam does a better job of his little "ask me something only I would know" game than Kayla did the first time around.

I decide to come right out with it.

"Sam wanted me to give you a message."

"What?" she says, pulling her hands closer to her body, mouth hanging open, waiting for my response.

"He came to me at the first grief meeting I went to, again at the one I went to with my wife, and now again tonight, asking me to give you a message. I don't know how I can see him and you can't, and I don't expect you to believe me, but ... "

She puts her hand over her trembling lips. Her eyes watered. "He *came* to you?"

Already I can tell that she's not like Meg. She seems to be looking for a reason *to believe*. Perhaps she's a little too eager, the kind of person that so-called psychics would bleed for every penny.

"Yes, he wanted me to tell you that he didn't mean to kill himself."

She stared at me. "He what?"

I look at Sam, who is also crying now, and ask, "What was the rest, Sam?"

He tells me, and I convey the message.

"He says that he just wanted to get sick enough to stay home from school for a while, but he didn't think he'd die. At most, he thought he might get in trouble, and you'd have to keep him home because you were afraid he might do something like this again."

"He's here?" she asks, looking where I'm looking.

"Yes," I say. "He says that he's so sorry that you blamed yourself after he died. And he said, please don't do what you said you'd do."

"What do you mean?"

I ask Sam, who is now crying more than his mother. He can barely get the words out, and as he does they hit me right in the heart.

I can hardly look at her as I say this, but I have to see if what he said is true. Her eyes will tell me and confirm, again, that he's truly here telling me these things. And if he *is* here, then that means Kayla is also waiting for me at home.

"Sam says that after you tried to revive him and realized that you were too late, you begged God to take you, too. And that on many nights you say to yourself that you'll join him soon."

Kathy stares at me, and then at Sam's ghost.

Her eyes widen. "Sam?"

"You see him?"

Sam asks her, too.

"Yes, baby, I see you," A smile spreads across Kathy's trembling lips as she reaches out to touch him. Her hands rest on his shoulders, as if he's there, solid and real.

My heartbeat is racing as I wonder if I'll have this sort of reunion with Kayla.

They embrace.

Sam says, "Please, Mama, don't kill yourself. It wasn't your fault. It was an accident. The man in black says I won't go to hell for an accident. And I don't want you to kill yourself and wind up in hell without me."

She doesn't ask who the man in black is. All she does is hold him, crying over and over, "I won't, honey, I won't."

Kathy's hands suddenly slip through Sam as he begins to fade.

*No! He can't leave now. He has to tell me what Kayla said to him.*

"I have to go now, Mama."

"Wait," I say, "I need you to tell me what Kayla said!"

He looks at me. "She can tell you. You just need to see her."

He's fading more, almost gone, his voice trailing away.

"How can I see her?" I shout.

"Take more—" and then he is gone, without finishing his sentence.

*Take more what?*

"No!" I yell, leaping from the table as if I can grab him and keep him here.

Kathy stumbles back and almost falls. I reach out and manage to keep her steady.

She looks up at me. "Where did he go?"

"He moved on. He said that once he delivered his message to you he could go where he was supposed to."

"To heaven?"

"Yes," I say, not that he'd ever told me. But if it comforts her, then it seems right to say.

I stand there, staring at the spot where Sam had just been, unable to believe that he vanished before delivering his promise.

Kathy asks, "What are you talking about with Kayla? Did you see your daughter, too?"

"No, Sam did. He said if I helped him move on, he'd help her talk to me, so she can move on, too."

Kathy asks, "What does 'take more' mean?"

It dawns on me. The only thing it can mean.

"I think it means take more pills."

I look at her and realize that I need to get home. Now.

"I'm sorry," I say, walking past her without waiting for her to lead me out, "I need to get home."

"Thank you, Tom!" Kathy calls out.

"You're welcome," I say, rushing out her front door and racing to my car.

# Chapter Fourteen

I ARRIVE HOME at 3:15 a.m., and run into the house, screaming her name.

"Kayla?"

I don't see or hear her.

I go to my office and grab my pills, then to the fridge for a bottle of water, talking to her all the while, hoping she is here and can hear me.

"I helped Sam move on. I told him what his mother wanted to know, and then … you won't believe this … but she saw him and talked with him, for just a moment. Then he was gone."

I carry the bottles upstairs, heading toward Kayla's bedroom.

I push the door open, flick on the pink light, and sit on her bed.

"If you're trying to talk to me right now, I can't hear or see you. And Sam disappeared before he could tell me what you wanted him to tell me. But he said I can see you. I just need to 'take more.' The only thing that makes sense to me is that he wants me to take more of the pain pills.

They precipitated a lot of this, I think. I'm not sure why, but these pills helped me see him. And I think they allowed me to hear you, too, but only when I was sleeping. I figure if I take more — not too many, don't worry — but if I take more, maybe I'll be able to see you."

I unscrew the pill bottle and pour three into my hand. A good start, I figure, as I wash the pills down with water.

I kick off my shoes and lean back on her bed, feeling the softness of her cool pillow melt beneath my head. I smell her shampoo again, and I wonder if the scent is in the pillow, as I'd thought before, or if perhaps she's in the room right now.

*Ghosts don't have scents, though, do they?*

I don't remember Sam smelling one way or another. I only remember the cold.

I start talking, hoping she's in the room.

"Do you remember when you were eight months old?" I ask, looking at the doll I bought her, still on the night-stand, untouched.

There's no answer, so I close my eyes and continue.

"You woke up in the middle of the night with a high fever. I don't remember what it was, but Meg said it was dangerously bad. And you were coughing this horrible croupy cough. I was so scared. Your mom bundled you up and carried you to the car, and then I drove us about 80 miles an hour to the emergency room. The doctor was running all these tests on you, and then she needed to do chest X-Rays. She took you from me, and you were screaming so loud, looking up at me with wounded eyes, like, 'Why did you give me to this lady? Why aren't you helping me, Daddy?', and I had to just sit there as she was doing the X-Rays. You kept screaming, and even though I knew in the logical part of my mind that she wasn't hurting you, in my heart it was killing me. I wanted to snatch you back from her, and tell her to keep her hands off of you. At one point, I thought I might hit her."

I open my eyes to see if I have company, but I don't.

Nor do I feel anything from the pills yet.

I sit up and open the bottle and take two more, along with another swallow of water.

I lie back down and continue my story.

"I remember realizing right then and there how truly helpless I was. No matter what precautions I took or how well I raised you, someday something could happen. Maybe you'd get beaten up by some bully at school. Some boy might treat you poorly. Or maybe we'd get into a car accident, and ... " I can't finish the sentence.

I wipe the tears from my eyes.

I can feel the emotions swelling in my head. The pills are starting to work, though I'm not feeling joy. Only a profound sorrow.

"Remember how you used to stand outside my door when I was writing? You'd sit there trying to lure me away from my desk, making funny faces, or sometimes playing on my sympathy with a sad face, and telling me how you just wanted me to sit with you?"

I wipe more tears away, feeling the sting of memories cutting like razors.

"And I always said, 'Hold on,' or 'In a few minutes,' or whatever I had to say to get a few more uninterrupted minutes writing. And then you'd slink away feeling dejected, wounded. I don't know if you know I noticed when you went away, or maybe thought I was so into my work that I didn't even notice, or care. But I did, Kayla. I knew each and every time you walked away from my door, because it hurt like hell to not get up and chase you, to go spend time with you. But I knew if I did, I'd be making it that much harder to return to the story. I'd be setting you up to expect me to just drop what I'm doing, and I couldn't."

I laugh at myself, making excuses and defending my actions even after Kayla is dead.

"I'm sorry, Kayla. I'd trade every page of every book I ever wrote to have you back. To go back in time and get up from my desk to sit with you."

Suddenly, a flash of memory:

I'm driving in my car, on a hot summer morning.

It's the day of the accident, though I'm not sure how I know.

I look in the back seat to see Kayla, smiling at me. She has her lunchbox, all ready for school. In the mirror, I see the light again, like a glare, a reflection of something in the back seat beside her.

*What is it?*

The flash is gone, quick like Sam's vanishing.

His words echo in my head.

*Just take more.*

I sit up and look around. Still no sign of Kayla in her room. I fish two more pills from the bottle and swallow them.

I lie back down.

I want to apologize more for not being there, but every word is hollow from my lips. Words mean nothing when they come too late. It's what you do when your child is alive that matters. Not now.

I turn over in her bed, crying into her pillow.

I just want this pain to end. I feel it coursing over me like a flood that will surely take me with it, choke me, drown me, drag me to the depths of nothingness. I wonder how many more pills it would take to end the pain for good?

"Daddy?" I hear her voice as a hand softly touches my head.

A cold chill runs through me at the touch.

I turn, quickly, and see her sitting on the edge of the bed, looking at me with her head tilted sideways.

"Kayla?" I ask, reaching out to touch her face.

My fingers meet her cheek's smooth surface.

My mouth opens, tears pouring from my eyes, as I stare at the impossible.

"Daddy?" she says, still looking up at me. "Can you hear me?"

"I hear you."

I want to wrap my arms around her and hug her hard. Never let her go. Damn the man in black, those ghost things, or Jesus Christ himself. Nobody will ever separate us again. They'll have to take me with her. But as I try to hug her, my arms refuse to cooperate. I can't move them.

I'm confused. And the pain I was feeling before is now like a knife in my head, like a migraine on steroids.

She looks at me in that same odd way. "Daddy, are you awake?"

*Awake?*

"I'm right here," I say. "I'm right here. Can't you see me? Or hear me?"

She turns away from me, like she's talking to someone else behind her, someone I can't see.

"I think he's awake!" she says. "Come here!"

*Who is she talking to?*

*Is Sam with her? Another ghost?*

The door behind her is closed, and suddenly I'm afraid who might walk through.

"Who are you talking to, Kayla?"

And then she's gone.

I reach out, desperate to feel something. But she's not there.

"Kayla?" I cry, the pain now feeling as if it's moving like an actual blade through my brain, like a parasite searching for the rawest part of me to bore into.

I reach for the pills, pop two more into my mouth, hoping they'll make the pain subside and bring Kayla back into sight.

I wait, sitting on her bed, hoping against hope that she'll appear again.

"Please, Kayla," I cry.

The room is getting warmer, almost unbearably hot, reminding me of the summer flashback I'd had moments ago.

I hear something, the sound of clicking in the distance. I remember the horrible things that had come through the school hallway.

*Had they been clicking?*

I can't remember.

*Have they found me?*

*Have they come for Kayla?*

*Did they sense her getting upset?*

*Or, perhaps, me?*

"Keep calm, Kayla," I say, assuming she's still here, "If you're calm they can't see you."

I jump up from Kayla's bed, stuff the pill bottle into my pocket, then head into the hallway. Lights flicker overhead. They go out for good, plunging the hall into black.

I stop in my tracks, the blade in my head digging impossibly deeper.

I cry out in pain and fall to the floor, vomiting in the darkness.

Hot puke splashes my arms, and I hope I didn't lose the pills. I need them in my system. I need to see her again.

I feel along the wooden floor, hands slipping through my stomach's squishy contents, searching for the hard shape of pills in my mess. I'll take more, but only if I puked up the others. Too many will mean an overdose for sure.

I try and remember how many I've taken, to see if I can swallow more without risk of death.

*Fuck, I can't remember.*

I continue feeling in the darkness, searching through the mess, then my finger runs into something hard. Something that feels like … a shoe. A man's shoe.

I look up but see nothing.

I run my hands up, feeling pants and legs.

"Who's there?" I ask, stumbling back on all fours, slipping in my puke.

"You know who I am," the man says, his whisper like velvet in the darkness. It feels like it's right next to my ear, even though he's standing a good two feet in front of me now.

"The man in black?" I ask, as it's the only thing that comes to mind.

"Yes," he says.

The lights flicker, and I look up to see the man from the photographs. I only see him for a second, but immediately I notice his eyes, glowing blue. And … an almost pleasant smile.

"Who are you?"

"Who is not as important as why I'm here."

"*Why* are you here?" I ask.

"Because you're not supposed to be."

"What does *that* mean?"

"You were supposed to die, but you didn't. And now … well, now you're here. You can't stay here, Tom. This place isn't for you."

"What do you mean? Not for me? Where's my daughter?"

The lights go black again, and I reach out, but he's no longer there.

*What does he mean I was supposed to have died? Is that why he's here? To take my soul? To bring me to heaven, hell, or wherever it is we go when we die?*

Terror floods my body.

I don't want to go.

I'm not ready to go.

I'm shivering, cold.

The lights in the hall are flickering again, just enough for me to see that the man in black is gone. I look down between the strobes of darkness and light, probing the floor for any sign of pills. I see none in my vomit, which means they're probably all still inside me.

I probably shouldn't take more.

I suppose no more are needed, though, if I'm getting a visit from the man in black. I try to tell myself that this is all in my head, that I should just wake up, and everything will be fine.

But nothing about that statement feels real.

The hallway is plunged into darkness again. Outside, thunder is booming, and rain starts hitting the windows in the rooms on either side of me hard.

I open the door to my right, Kayla's room, and see just enough moonlight coming through her windows to make out the bottle of water I left on her bed. I call out for her again.

"Kayla?"

Suddenly, the clicking sound again. It's mostly muted, as if it's happening just under the floor, or maybe in the walls.

"Daddy," I hear.

"Kayla?" I call out.

I can't see her.

"Daddy," she says again, this time a bit louder, and I realize she's not in her room. She sounds like she's coming from the guest room at the end of the hall. Beneath that door, light flickers on and off. Or perhaps it's lightning, as thunder crashes through the hallway, reminding my brain of the blade twisting through it.

I reach into my pocket, grab the bottle, take two more pills, swallow them.

I think about going back to Kayla's room for the bottle of water, but she calls for me again.

"Daddyyyy!" this time a shrill scream, like someone is hurting her.

I run to the end of the hall, and seize the doorknob.

It burns my hand, like the doorknob in my dream.

Makes me think that maybe I'm dreaming now.

*Please, God, let me be dreaming.*

"Daddy!" she screams again from the other side, "Wake up, Daddy!"

"I am awake!" I yell, clutching the knob in my hand, despite the burning, trying to twist it open. It's not locked, but it's barely moving, as if rusted or something.

I twist, the heat like fire burning into my flesh as if I'm trying to twist off a lit stove burner.

I let go.

Lightning flashes in the room beyond.

Kayla screams.

I launch myself shoulder first into the door.

It bursts open.

I stumble forward into the room, tumbling through darkness to the ground, hitting my head on a dresser I don't recall being there.

I rise to my feet as the light flickers on and off. Between

the flashes, I look around, at first for Kayla, and then at the room itself.

This isn't my guest room.

Dark.

Light — I see that there's no bed.

Dark.

Light — instead, there's a crib.

Dark.

Light — a changing table.

Dark.

Light — and a name in wooden letters on the wall over the crib.

Dark.

Light — it says, *Sam*.

And then I remember.

# Chapter Fifteen

I'M DRIVING on a summer morning, too damned hot for such an early hour. They say the summers are getting worse, and that we should all just get used to it.

Kayla's in the backseat, holding her lunchbox, ready for school.

Beside her is my six-month old son, Sam, in the car seat, playing with his little stuffed yellow bear.

We're running late.

Meg is sick, and I'm running the kids to school and daycare before going into the city to meet Marty so we can figure out what to do about this shit contract that the publisher expects us to sign for the next two books in the *Dark Family* series.

With the third book we're working on, our contractual obligation is up. They're trying to sign us to another three, but the terms, especially on the e-book rights, are shit. At the same time, we're negotiating with a producer who may be able to bring a decent version of the series to TV. But there are politics involved, a lot of glad-handing and ass kissing. The kind of stuff that Marty is good at, which I suck at, and which just frustrates Meg to no end. Perhaps that's why she's sick. Not saying she's faking. But I think anxiety got her defenses down, and one thing led to another, and now I'm taking this trip into Manhattan alone.

She suggested I fly, but I hate flying — even if it's a short flight — only slightly more than I hate these meetings. So I said I'd drop Kayla off at school and Sam at daycare, then she can pick them up if my meetings run late.

I pull up in front of Kayla's school and see another mother we know, Mrs. Sutton, with her daughter, Felicia, also in Kayla's class, walking past our car. Mrs. Sutton sometimes volunteers as a helper in the class, so perhaps she can save me fifteen minutes of having to find a parking spot and cart Sam in, then bringing him back out and fastening him down in the car seat again. He's quiet now, drinking his bottle; I hate to aggravate him.

I roll down the window and call out, "Hey, Mrs. Sutton?"

She comes up to my car. "Hi, Tom, how are you?"

The girls wave at one another, giggly as Kayla hops out of the car and says hi to her friend.

"Good, how are you?"

"Great, I see you got car duties today." She knows I hate taking the kids to school.

"Yeah, Meg is sick," I say using air quotes to joke that she's playing hooky. "Listen. I need to run into the city, and I'm running late. Could you take Kayla to class?"

"Sure," she says, smiling. I like Mrs. Sutton, even if I can't remember her first name. I know Meg also likes her. I think they've had a few play dates with the kids, though I could be confusing her for someone else.

"Thank you, I appreciate it."

I open my door to hug Kayla goodbye, "You have a good day in school, OK?"

"OK, Daddy. Will you be home for dinner?"

"I don't know," I say, anticipating the disappointment that follows. "I'll try my best. And if not, I'll make it up to you."

"How?" she asks, smiling coyly.

Meg hates when I bargain with the kids or promise things I won't deliver. But just this once won't hurt.

"I'll write you a story."

"Maybe you can help Mommy write that porcupine story I asked her to write?"

"Porcupine story?" I ask. Before she can give me details, I see the clock, and realize I should really get going. "Oh, yeah, the porcupine story. Yes, I'll help Mommy write it if I'm not back in time for dinner."

"Promise?"

"Promise," I say, even though I have no idea what story she's talking about, then hug and kiss her goodbye.

She opens the rear door, leans in, and kisses Sam on the forehead, "Bye, baby brother," she says.

"He's sooooo cute," her friend says.

Kayla says bye again and closes the rear door.

"Thanks again," I say to Mrs. Sutton as I pull away. I wave goodbye to Kayla, and then head out of the parking lot, looking to make up for lost time.

I look back at the car seat to see Sam giving me a big goofy smile.

I love his smile. He's only recently started giving what I think are genuine smiles. I used to think he was smiling all the time, because whenever I'd feed him or rock him to sleep, he'd look back and give me these big grins. Meg said they were probably just gas, though.

I'm not sure if she was busting my balls, or not, but this

smile on his face now is the kind of happy smile that a son only gives his Daddy. Or maybe his Mommy, too.

"Just you and me, Sam," I say, heading to his daycare.

He lets out a babble that sounds like "Da."

~

12:25 p.m.

I'm sitting in Marty's office, staring at page after page of legalese in his proposed counteroffer to the publisher, enough to make my head swim.

After a long drive into the city, then waiting forever for Marty (who was running late with another client) then spending forty minutes bullshitting about the Yankees, I'm tired, and hungry, and wishing I'd thought to bring something to eat.

"I'm not gonna lie," I say, "I can't think straight right now. Long night, woke up early to take the kids to school, and I'm starving. Can we finish talking about this over a late lunch?"

"Hell yeah," Marty says. "Wanna do Harry's Pub?"

"Yeah," I say, "let's do that."

We get up to leave, and suddenly my phone is ringing with a call from Meg, rather than buzzing from a text.

I wonder why she's calling, and then immediately think that one of the kids is probably sick and needs to be picked up early. She better not ask me to leave the city before lunch. She'll have to cover this one on her own.

I pick up the phone. "Hey, baby."

She cuts past the pleasantries, voice distressed, "Is Sam with you?"

"What do you mean is Sam with me? I dropped him off at daycare."

"I just called them, to check up on him since they

usually call me at nap time on the days we bring him, and they said you never dropped him off."

"Of course I did," I say, though doubt creeps into my voice as I try to think back.

*Didn't I?*

I retrace my steps. I'd been in such a rush, I don't remember much after dropping Kayla off at school with Mrs. Sutton.

I dropped him off.

*Didn't I?*

But I can't remember for certain. My mind was so clouded with the day ahead, the contract talks, and all I needed to do when I got home, I can't remember much of anything that I actually did for certain.

*Oh God.*

"I'll call you back," I say, hanging up and racing from Marty's office.

I go to the elevators and hit the call button. Both elevators are on the first floor. I'm on the fourteenth. I can't wait.

I run to the stairs, descending them two at a time, racing to the parking lot as fast as I can. The stairwell grows hotter with each floor I pass, as I'm sweating through my shirt.

*I had to have dropped Sam off at daycare. Right?*

*But if he's not there, where the hell is he?*

My first thought is that someone took him. Someone kidnapped my child, and they're going to ask for a ransom. I knew we should've hired bodyguards the minute the *Dark Family* series took off. Some assholes want to get paid, and they don't care who they hurt to get theirs.

No problem. I'll pay whatever they want. Nothing is more important than getting Sam back.

I hit the tenth floor and am struggling to keep my pace and catch my breath.

*What if it's not ransom? What if some pervert took Sam?*

Seventh floor.

I can't even fathom that. It happens all the time, at least according to the news reports. But that happens to other people, not to you.

*Not to my family.*

Second floor, one more to go.

I hit the first floor, gasping for air as my phone starts ringing in my pocket.

I don't answer. I race outside and out into the parking lot beneath the bright summer sun.

I'm searching for my car, trying to remember where the hell I parked.

There it is, at the end of the row.

I run, ignoring the ringing in my pocket.

I finally reach the car. My heart stops in my chest.

*Oh God.*

*Oh God, no.*

I fumble for my keys, click unlock, and before I even open the door I know I'm too late.

Sam is dead, boiled alive in the car.

*ONE MONTH LATER ...*

I'm sitting outside on the hotel room balcony, staring up at the moon, half-empty bottle of vodka in hand.

Behind me, I hear the late night news come on, a regurgitation of what I already watched two hours ago.

I listen as my story leads the half hour.

The news anchor talks about how the sheriff decided today not to press charges in the death of my son "which rocked not just the small town of Warrenville, but the publishing world."

The anchor cuts to an interview with Sheriff John Martin, who says, "It's a terrible tragedy what happened, but it's also an accident. We feel that we can't possibly punish Mr. Witt any more than the hell he and his family are already going through. It's a tough call, but I believe it's the right one."

The anchor then talks to some loudmouth who goes on about how I got special treatment because I'm a "celebrity."

I'm not sure how long I'll be in this hotel, but Marty said it was a best to stay here under a pseudonym until the heat dies down.

Meg and Kayla are staying with her sister until it's safe to return home without being hounded by the press. At least that's what she told me. But for all I know, she may decide to stay gone forever.

How can she ever forgive me what I've done?

*I can't* forgive me after what I've done.

No matter how many times I replay the events in my head, it doesn't make sense.

How could I forget my son was in the car?

I was so damned distracted by these fucking book and TV deals that I forgot to drop him off at daycare.

He must've fallen asleep after the bottle.

And then I drove four hours to see Marty.

Four hours, and he didn't wake up.

Four hours, and I forgot my child was in the back seat.

I play his final moments over and over in my head. He must've woken, wondering where his daddy was. Cried for me.

And then, as the sun grew hotter, and he began to

cook, Sam must've screamed, struggling to get out of his car seat, crying out for someone to come help him.

Confused, wondering what was happening.

*Dying from the fucking heat.*

I reach into my lap, grab the pain pills I got following the incident. Told the doc I was getting these horrible headaches. It was true. I was. But now they help to numb the pain. I pop two in my mouth, and swallow more vodka.

*SIX MONTHS LATER ...*

I'm sitting in the car, watching cold rain drizzle down the windows as I sit outside my house. The wipers thump rhythmically, making me sleepy. Making me wish *I could* sleep for more than a few hours at a time these days.

I want to go inside and kiss my wife and daughter.

I want to sit down to dinner like we used to.

But nothing is the same.

It never will be.

We're together under one roof, ghosts of ourselves, a family in name only.

Meg is struggling to get through this. We're doing therapy twice a week. Kayla's also in therapy, though she seems to be taking this better than any of us. She's sad that her brother's gone. She knows that I'm to blame, but she, of all people, seems most ready to forgive me.

But Meg can't.

Nor can I.

I am a burden to them. I can feel it in the way Meg looks at me. She hates me, and wishes it were me that was dead. She doesn't say anything so mean, of course. She's too kind for that.

But I see it in her eyes.

I feel it in her touch, on the rare occasions that we have physical contact.

I sit outside my house, a stranger.

I don't know how long I can go on with this charade of pretending to be the man I used to be. How much easier it would've been had the sheriff prosecuted me. At least then I wouldn't be this constant reminder in Meg's and Kayla's lives of the man who killed Baby Sam.

I've been taking more pills to try and make the pain go away, but it only makes the pain deeper and longer, and the brief moments of joy — my daughter's smile or laugh, a moment where things feel almost like they once were — more fleeting.

Meg doesn't deserve this constant reminder of our tragedy.

Nor does Kayla.

I pull out of the driveway as the rain begins to pour harder, the sky splitting open in a torrent of gray.

I've already decided what to do, but I can't tell them. If Meg knows, there's no way she'd be able to lie through the inevitable investigation.

I can't leave a note.

I can't get loaded on drugs or alcohol to make it easier. I just have to do it.

They'll get a nice insurance settlement that should take care of them comfortably for a long time.

I consider calling Marty to let him know. I know *he* can keep a secret. But I don't want to put that burden on him to keep such a secret from Meg. He's a good man — a better man than me — and I don't have to ask him to take care of my family. He just will.

I drive out of my neighborhood, head out to the highway, then make a couple of turns to get back on the same stretch, but the opposite way so it seems like I was on my way home.

So it seems like an accident.

I want to call Meg and Kayla to hear their voices once more, to tell them I love them.

But I can't be selfish.

I just have to do this.

For them.

I speed up, making sure not to go *too fast*. The insurance might not cover my death if I'm speeding.

I see the guardrail ahead. The one I'd noticed was broken two weeks ago. The one over the steep ravine.

I position my car in the middle lane, waiting for the right moment. The moment that I can get over, then hit the brakes so it appears that I tried to stop rather than sped up and plunged myself off the road.

Two cars behind me, and a truck in the middle lane.

Adrenaline pumps through me as I steady myself to do what every part of my body is screaming for me not to do.

The rail is rapidly approaching.

I speed up to fifty-five, then merge, a bit too far.

The car fishtails as I slam on the brakes.

No stopping now. The car hydroplanes right through the broken guardrail, and I plunge downward.

The last thing I think of as I brace for impact is my sweet son's face and how he'd smiled at me that morning.

A smile betrayed.

~

I SHOULD BE DEAD.

Instead, there's a lot of noise and movement over me.

My whole body is in pain, and I can't move.

I look up, eyes blurred, and see a female police officer

asking me something. Her voice is garbled and sounds like she's under water.

I try to talk, but can't.

My eyes swim over her face, then settle on her badge: *Ruiz*.

She yells something to someone.

Darkness swallows me.

# Chapter Sixteen

I'M BACK in my house, present day, in Sam's room, after remembering everything.

The pain of remembering is too much to bear. It feels like I had him, raised him for six months, and then lost him all over again. I'm crying, looking around the now-lit room. The lights have stopped flickering, and everything seems normal, though there's a slight dreamlike feel to the world that I can't shake.

*Am I really here?*

*Or am I in some kind of hell or purgatory?*

My memories are all jumbled, dream, reality, memory. I can't be certain of anything except that Sam is dead, and it's all my fault.

*Poor Sam. How can a father forget his son in a car?*

It seems impossible, yet it happens all too often. But that's to other people.

Not to me.

Not to us.

I look around Sam's lit room, untouched since the accident. Neither Meg nor I can bring ourselves to change the nursery just yet.

"Daddy, are you awake?" I hear Kayla's voice behind me.

I turn, expecting to see her ghost in the doorway, but then remember she's alive. All those memories of the accident with her were false, an accident that never happened. *Did it? Or were there two accidents?*

I can't remember anything after Ruiz found me. Nothing real, anyway.

"Daddy? Are you awake?" Kayla asks again, her voice sounding even closer.

My heart pounding hopeful in my chest, I go to the door and open it, but Kayla's not there.

*So, how am I hearing her?*

*Where am I?*

The man in black steps into the hall, coming from her room, his bright-blue eyes looking me up and down. "Do you remember now?"

"Yes," I say, wiping tears from my eyes. "What's happening to me?"

"You're in a coma, Tom. You tried to kill yourself."

The way he says the words 'kill yourself,' it sounds almost as if he's judging me.

"Who are you?"

He doesn't answer. Instead, he puts a hand to his ear, cupping it. "You can hear her, can't you?"

"Kayla?" I ask.

"Yes, she's sitting in a hospital room right now, waiting for her Daddy to wake up. And Meg is there waiting, too."

"How long have I been out?"

"Long enough to spin this elaborate fiction around a truth you couldn't face. That is some world-class lying to yourself there, son. No wonder you're a writer."

I shake my head.

He continues, "You've also been gone long enough that the doctors are starting to give up on you. If you don't respond soon, you may never wake up. Once you pass a year, the odds of returning to anything resembling normal are astronomically against you."

"Good," I say. "They're better off without me."

"*Who's* better off without you?"

"Them," I say, "you know who I'm talking about."

"Say their names, Tom."

I look at the man in black, wanting to punch his smug face.

*Who the hell is he to talk to me like this?*

I look at him, annoyed. I want to yell at him, ask him how the hell he knows what's happening in my head, but I assume he's just one more elaborate fiction fashioned by me. I'm arguing with my subconscious.

But looking into his bright-blue eyes, I can't help but feel like I'm in the presence of something else — something close to an angel, if I believed in such things.

*Man, they must have me on some excellent meds.*

"Say their names, Tom," he repeats. "Who is better off without you?"

"Meg and Kayla," I say.

The man in black shakes his head, lips pursed. More judgment.

He says, "You've been trying so hard to remember what you forgot in the accident. And you were so eager to have your daughter back in your arms when you thought you'd lost her, but now ... what? You just give up? I thought you were so much stronger than this. But I guess it's true what they say about suicides being selfish cowards."

"I'm not a coward," I yell. "I was trying to help them.

They got insurance money. They wouldn't have to see this constant reminder of the life we *could've* had. The life I fucked up! I killed him! I killed my son! What kind of monster does such a thing? Forgets his son in the back of a hot car? What kind?"

I break down, unable to say more. I just want the man in black gone.

Let me return to the fiction I created. Perhaps I can do better with the next iteration — spin a world where I have my daughter *and* my son, and my wife, and we all live happily ever after.

The man in black won't shut up, though. "So, this is better? Your wife and daughter watching you slowly creep toward death? Waiting for you to wake up, and holding out hope against hope that you'll beat the odds? That you'll be one of the people who comes out of a coma and can live a normal life again? But you choose to reject them — choose to be selfish and die rather than stay and fight. They come here every day, waiting for you to wake up, man. If that isn't love, I don't know what is."

"Daddy, are you awake?" Kayla asks again. "I swear, he was awake. He looked at me and talked to me. He said my name."

I hear machines beeping, the sound of something else clicking, all of it sounding almost as if it's underwater.

Meg asks, "Are you sure he said your name, Kayla?"

"I swear, Mom, he said my name."

"You know that sometimes Daddy seems to be awake, but he's really not, right? The doctor told us about that, remember?"

"He *was* awake!" Kayla yells.

The man in black comes closer, "Are you going to prove your daughter right, Tom? You have the power to wake up now, and rejoin the world. Or you can stay here in this … *whatever you've created here* … living out these lies."

"I want to wake up," I say, "but I don't want any more pain. I don't want to cause *them* any more pain."

The man meets my eyes, and seems to be almost staring through them, into my soul. "Life is full of pain, Tom. Do you remember when you brought your daughter to the hospital with the croup? Remember how scared you were, and how mad you were at that X-ray technician who held her in the machine?"

"Yes," I say.

"But that's not the part of the story you remember most, is it?"

I look at him, wondering what he means.

"You remember the after, right? When you held Kayla in your arms again, comforting her, telling her how much you loved her and that she'd be OK."

I nod yes.

"If you don't wake up, there won't be an after. This will be the last thing your family remembers, and you'll never have a chance to tell them how much you love them, or that you'll all be OK."

"Will we?" I ask. "Will we be OK?"

"There's only one way to find out, Tom. There are no guarantees in any of this. But you've been given something most people would kill for — a second chance. But you must wake up."

"How?" I ask, tears streaming down my cheeks.

I try to imagine myself waking, but nothing's happening.

"Daddy?" Kayla's voice calls again, sounding even farther away.

"Come on," Meg says. "We need to get home."

"I want to wait for Daddy," Kayla says.

"We have to go, honey."

"Daddy, please, wake up," Kayla cries. The sound of her crying feels like a knife in my gut, twisting harsher because I can't answer her.

I try to wake again, but nothing's happening.

"How do I wake up?" I yell at the man in black as I hear Kayla crying, "I don't want to go."

Meg says, "We have to, we'll come back tomorrow."

But I know there won't be a tomorrow. Not if I don't seize it now.

"How do I wake up?" I yell again.

The man meets my eyes, "You must *want to* live."

"I want to!" I yell.

"Don't tell me, tell them."

I hear Meg pulling Kayla outside the door.

*No! Don't leave!*

I wake with a scream.

I'm in the hospital room, hooked to machines, tubes running through my nose, seeing the door swing shut.

I'm too late.

I want to get up and chase them, but my body refuses to obey.

I'm too late.

And then the door swings open.

Meg and Kayla stand in the doorway, eyes wide in shock.

They heard me.

"Daddy?"

I look into Kayla's eyes and then Meg's, both of them filled with tears as they try to believe the impossible.

I try to talk, but can't form the words I'm longing to say — to let them know how much I love them.

But as they come toward me, and embrace me, I realize I don't need to say anything.

They already know.

## THE END

## What to Read Next

If you loved reading *Crash*, you should definitely go get *Monstrous* and start reading the *Monstrous* series today.

Get Monstrous Today

# A Quick Favor

Thank you for reading *Crash*.

If you enjoyed this book please consider writing a review of it on your favorite bookseller so other readers might enjoy it too. Just a couple of sentences would mean a lot to me.

Thank you!

# Author's Note

---

Hello there, Dear Reader. Here's the part of the book where I tell you a bit about my inspiration for *Crash* and why we wanted to write a standalone story as opposed to the series books we're known for.

If you're the kind of person that likes to skip straight to the Author's Note first, I suggest you turn back as this WILL CONTAIN SPOILERS!

You have been warned.

While Sean and I are known for our series work, we've got a LOT of stories in our heads — things we want to bring into this world — we're not going to create series for them all!

For one, not every story *should* be a series.

Two, it's hard enough to manage six series, let alone add more to the plate. We pretty much decided not to start any new series until we close out a few (starting with $Z$ *2136* which ended the $Z$ trilogy for 47North).

And then there's some readers who don't really like series, not until they're all wrapped and done, anyway.

Those people have been waiting for us to do a proper book — with a beginning and end!

So we decided to dip into our story garden and write two standalone titles during a brief break between our other series work.

We each had these ghost story-type novels we wanted to write.

The idea was that we'd each take lead on our own idea, and then we'd work together on the edits (like we do with our *Dark Crossings* stories).

We figured we'd take a month, two tops, to write our books.

That was last summer!

Turns out that these two titles took longer than any other project we've written!

I'll let Sean tell his story about *Threshold* in his Author's Note when the book comes out next month. But here's a bit of the behind-the-scenes on why I took so long to write *Crash*.

First, though, we have to talk about the origins of this story.

The original version of *Crash*, which I conceived in 1988, was about a writer who was in an accident which nearly killed him, and left his girlfriend in a coma. In fact, I was going to call it *Girlfriend in a Coma*, which a year earlier had been a Smiths song (though I didn't hear of it until I had cooler taste in music than I did in the 80s). Later, in 1998, Douglas Coupland wound up writing a book of that title, which made me drop it.

Anyway, back to *my* story premise — Thomas Witt spent his waking hours by his girlfriend's side in a hospital where he … (*wait for it*) … saw dead people.

He helped these dead people finish their unfinished business. He even solved an ancient murder at the hospital.

And the end of the story came with the twist that Thomas Witt was dead all along.

It was going to be so damned awesome an ending. Nobody would expect it!

But then the movie *The Sixth Sense* came out and I felt like M. Night Shyamalan had reached into my head and stole my story!

I was soooooo pissed.

I ditched my book idea for a long time after that.

Sean and I have a recurring disagreement about what happens if we write something and then find out afterwards (or after we start) that someone else did something similar. I'm tempted to trash the whole thing and start over, trying to be "original." He's of the opinion that if someone else does an idea before you, it's not a problem. You just write something better, or will, by virtue of being a different person with different experiences and tastes, *will* come up with something different enough that it won't be the same.

As many creators say, there are no *New Ideas*. It's what you *do* with the idea. How *you* make it different or new. What *you* bring to the story.

But every now and then there *is* an idea that is executed so well, like the ending of *The Sixth Sense*, that it becomes part of pop culture knowledge. And anyone who does anything even remotely close is either ripping it off or offering a weak homage to it.

That movie ruined my ability to write the story I originally thought up.

So I had to think of a different ending and change the story — a lot.

My back-up idea was that Thomas Witt was the one in a coma. He just *thought* his girlfriend was. I spent a lot of time researching comas, too, which gave me some cool ideas I wanted to include in the story. But that ending, too, felt like it had been done to death. That alone wouldn't work.

So I had to think of something else.

And I spent the next couple of decades writing parts of the story over and over, trying to come up with the right story, and ending.

I'm not usually about the big twist ending, but seeing as *Crash* started with one of the best twist ending ideas ever, long before it became cliche, I felt like this story needed something big — something that would shock people.

One idea I had was to have this big reveal that Tom, or perhaps his wife (no longer *just* his girlfriend), had been unfaithful. That seems like a pretty big thing that would be traumatic and hard to get past.

But it wasn't enough of a trauma. And it wasn't a terribly surprising twist.

I wanted to hit this family where it hurt most.

In 2007, my wife and I had our first son. And around this time, she got this sticker which reminds you not to leave your child in a car. Oddly, it was a one-sided sticker which faced outward. I thought it would've been better as a two-sided sticker or peel away to remind both other people *and the driver* of the message — "Hey, don't forget your kid!"

Because leaving children in a car *is* an avoidable tragedy. But it's also a fairly common one.

As impossible as it is to believe, people sometimes forget — even something as important as their child being in the car.

I can't imagine how I'd handle it if I'd done something like that. That would be the end of me, I think.

As I thought more about how tragic losing a child this way must be, I wanted to write about it. That's how I process things that terrify or anger me — I write.

I began to wonder — *What if this happened to my character, Tom Witt?*

I'm guessing that forgetting something like your child in the car feels like the ultimate betrayal of one's brain. I would imagine that anyone who has lived through this must be in constant torture and regret.

And I can't even imagine how it would feel to be the spouse of someone who did this. You're sad and angry. But how can you maintain an anger at someone who didn't mean to do it? Where do you, as the spouse, put your anger when it's a tragic mistake?

It's got to be the emptiest, most devastating feeling ever, something damned hard to come back from.

The more I thought about how tragic this ending was, the more I felt like I had to write it. It felt right for the story. This is a writer suffering from the greatest of all guilts and tragedies. One so horrible, he has blocked it off in his mind, created this false reality in his coma state.

In a way, this is even a better story than my original idea. This feels so much more real and raw than the "I see dead people" story I would've written.

And, to my knowledge, this particular story hasn't been done. Of course, I could be wrong. In which case, I'm blaming M. Night!

By the way, one of the reasons M. Night ruined my story isn't just that he did it first, but he did it so much better than I would have! *The Sixth Sense* is a masterpiece! I don't think I would've written something even half as good.

So, after many years of thinking and working on this story, last summer I sat down and started to properly write (and complete!) *Crash*, with this darker ending.

But then something happened while writing it.

I wondered if perhaps this ending was *too dark*?

Maybe there's a reason this story hasn't been written, or at least become a common story to tell.

It's tragic! It's dark. And nobody with children will want to read this book!

Halfway through the book, I froze, afraid to continue.

I didn't want to write something *this* dark.

I know that comes as surprising news to people who know of our penchant for putting children in jeopardy in Collective Inkwell stories!

But in a way, putting children, and adults, in jeopardy is our way of working through the things that scare us. It's cathartic. And there's always a bit of light at the end of the tunnel.

In this case, the light at the end of the tunnel was a train barreling towards the reader, the No Hope Express!

The ending was even too dark for me.

So I stalled, not wanting to write THIS ENDING, and the book continued to linger half done as I worked up the courage to finish it. And our regular readers wondered why the hell it was taking us so long to finish a single book? After all, we'd written a LOT over the course of the past two years. Why should one little story take so long?

After a month or so of inactivity on the title, I decided to start over. Not completely from scratch, but rather re-read the story and try and find what I was really trying to say with *Crash*.

A lot of what we write is fun, or we write it for thrills. But we don't typically have strong messages we're trying to deliver or Important Things to Say!

*Crash*, though, feels different.

I'm clearly trying to say something. A story doesn't demand to be written for nearly 30 years if you're not trying to say *something.* I knew it was about death.

I lost my best friend in an accident, and another person

I had been close to was murdered. Both of these things weighed heavily on me, in addition to losing family members.

What was I trying to say with this story?

What question was I putting out there?

I think a lot of the best stories ask a question. What you would do if this happened to you? What would you do in this situation?

As I was getting deeper into the story, I realized I wasn't writing about death. I was writing about fear.

And fear is something I've been dealing with for most of my life.

Yeah, I *thought* I was writing about death, but the story is about Tom being afraid to live with what he's done. He doesn't think he can be forgiven. He thinks his family will be better off without him. He doesn't want to screw things up again. And he can't stand the notion that he can't control fate — that he can't protect his family, least of all from himself.

It's almost easier for him to do nothing — to remain in a coma and live in blissful ignorance.

A feeling I think most people who live with anxiety and fear know all too well. Avoid the things that bring you pain, or *might* bring you pain, and just fly under the radar, and hope to get through life okay.

But what's the point of a life lived in fear?

If you avoid things like other people, experiences, and love, just because you're afraid then you've almost fulfilled your own fearful prophecies, right?

There's a scene near the climax of the book where the man in black is arguing with Tom, telling him that there's no guarantees in life. That the point of life isn't to avoid pain, but rather pick up and carry on, and to help others through it.

We can easily get lost in our own worlds, our own pains, our own loss, our own fears, and our own stories. The world can be a cruel place, especially for us sensitive souls.

But when we hide from the big cruel world, we risk losing sight of those closest to us — those who need us most, even in our flawed, fucked-up states. As messed up as *we* may be, there may be someone to whom we are the world. And we owe it to them, if not ourselves, to face our fears and act in spite of them.

Because in the end, our minutes here are limited. So far as we know, we only get to do this thing called Life one time.

To me, living in fear isn't really living. I feel like I've wasted far too many years living in fear. Time I will never get back. And that is a huge regret that can weigh on you as much as fear.

Would you rather spend your days living? Or hiding?

That is the question I wanted to ask with *Crash*. And while the ending is dark, I think there is a bit of hope there in what Tom chooses.

Thank you for joining us on this journey,

David Wright

# About the Authors

**Sean Platt** is an entrepreneur and founder of Sterling & Stone, where he makes stories with his partners, Johnny B. Truant, and David W. Wright, and a family of storytellers.

Sean is the bestselling author of over 10 million words' worth of books, including the Yesterday's Gone and Invasion series. Sean is also co-author of the indie publishing cornerstone, Write. Publish. Repeat. and co-host of the Story Studio Podcast.

Originally from Long Beach, California, Sean now lives in Austin, Texas with his wife and two children. He has more than his share of nose.

**David W. Wright** is the co-author of edge-of-your-seat thrillers including the best-selling post-apocalyptic series *Yesterday's Gone*, the paranoid sci-fi *WhiteSpace* series, and the vigilante series, *No Justice*, as well as standalone thrillers *12*, and *Crash* which was recently optioned for a movie.

David is an accomplished, though intermittent, cartoonist who lives in [LOCATION REDACTED] with his wife and son [NAMES REDACTED.]

He is not at all paranoid.

He is "the grumpy one" on *The Story Studio Podcast* with fellow Sterling and Stone founders, Sean Platt and Johnny B. Truant.

David writes about books, TV shows, movies, and

video games he enjoys; his struggles with anxiety and OCD; writing; and posts the occasional drawing at his personal blog at davidwwright.com

You can email him at david@sterlingandstone.net

We swear, he almost never bites. Unless you feed him after midnight.

For a full list of his most recent books visit sterlingandstone.net.

## Also By Sean Platt

**The Dead World Series**

Dead Zero

Dead City

Dead Nation

Dead Planet

Empty Nest

**The Beam Series**

The Beam Season One

The Beam Season Two

The Beam Season Three

**Robot Proletariat Series**

En3my

Robot Proletariat

The Infinite Loop

The Hard Reset

Cascade Failure

Reboot

**The Tomorrow Gene Series**

Null Identity

The Tomorrow Gene

The Tomorrow Clone

The Eden Experiment

## Karma Police Series

Jumper

Karma Police

The Collectors

Deviant

The Fall

Homecoming

## Yesterday's Gone

October's Gone

Yesterday's Gone Season One

Yesterday's Gone Season Two

Yesterday's Gone Season Three

Yesterday's Gone Season Four

Yesterday's Gone Season Five

Yesterday's Gone Season Six

## Tomorrow's Gone

Tomorrow's Gone Season One

Tomorrow's Gone Season Two

Tomorrow's Gone Season Three

## Available Darkness

Darkness Itself

Available Darkness Book One

Available Darkness Book Two

Available Darkness Book Three

## Also By David W. Wright

**Cold Vengeance**

Cold Vengeance

Cold Reckoning

**Hidden Justice**

Hidden Justice

Hidden Honor

Hidden Shame

Hidden Virtue

**No Justice**

No Justice

No Escape

No Hope

No Return

No Stopping

No Fear

**Karma Police**

Jumper

Karma Police

The Collectors

Deviant

The Fall

Homecoming

## Yesterday's Gone

October's Gone

Yesterday's Gone Season One

Yesterday's Gone Season Two

Yesterday's Gone Season Three

Yesterday's Gone Season Four

Yesterday's Gone Season Five

Yesterday's Gone Season Six

## Tomorrow's Gone

Tomorrow's Gone Season One

Tomorrow's Gone Season Two

Tomorrow's Gone Season Three

## Available Darkness

Darkness Itself

Available Darkness Book One

Available Darkness Book Two

Available Darkness Book Three

## WhiteSpace

WhiteSpace Season One

WhiteSpace Season Two

WhiteSpace Season Three

## Stand Alone Novels

Crash

Emily's List

Threshold

The Secret Within

www.ingramcontent.com/pod-product-compliance
Lightning Source LLC
Chambersburg PA
CBHW010543100726
47903CB00011B/3123